the
greatest
zombie
movie
ever

JEFF STRAND

sourcebooks
fire

Published by Sourcebooks Fire, an imprint of Sourcebooks, Inc.
P.O. Box 4410, Naperville, Illinois 60567-4410
(630) 961-3900
Fax: (630) 961-2168
www.sourcebooks.com

Library of Congress Cataloging-in-Publication data is on file with the publisher.

Printed and bound in the United States of America.
VP 10 9 8 7 6 5 4 3 2 1

This book is dedicated to past, current, and future generations of zombie fans. Yep, that should cover it.

WARNING!

THIS IS A BOOK ABOUT ZOMBIES.

If your immediate reaction is, "Books about zombies are evil! Eeeeeevil! Somebody hand me a bucket of lighter fluid so we can torch this sucker!" then this is probably not the book for you. That's fine. There are plenty of other books available for your reading enjoyment. In fact, Sourcebooks, the publisher of the novel that you were just talking about setting on fire, has a wide selection of non-zombie books, and I can pretty much guarantee that you'll find something that interests you. Thank you for reading this far. Perhaps we'll reconnect on a future novel.

Okay, they're gone. No, no, don't judge them. It's not their fault. Anyway, now it's time for the even more important warning...

This is not a book about real zombies.

I don't mean "real" as in "Aaahhh! Zombies exist!" I mean that the characters in this novel do not actually encounter the living dead. It's about kids making a zombie movie. I'm including this warning because I don't want you to start reading the book and think that it's about filmmakers who are going to use their zombie knowledge later when the *real* zombies attack. And then when you realize it's not going to happen, you scream in rage and fling the book (or the electronic device upon which you're reading it) across the room, hitting an innocent gerbil. Gerbils don't deserve this.

Is this a handy how-to guide for aspiring filmmakers? I don't know. *I* certainly wouldn't use it as one, but that might just be me.

Is it an inspiring tale about following your dreams even when the odds are against you? Hmmm. I'm reluctant to use the word "inspiring," for reasons that will become abundantly clear as you read this, but…you know what? I'm going to say yes on that one. So if you're mad that it doesn't have real zombies, you can stop breaking things long enough to appreciate the parts about following your dreams.

What it definitely is—and you've probably figured this out by now—is an extremely goofy comedy. Some people will even call it a stupid comedy. "That book was so dumb," they'll say, throwing their iPad into the trash. Good! Let them say it! No need for you to defend my honor. It's enough to know that *you* appreciate ridiculous literature.

To recap: Zombies. But not real zombies. Silly jokes.

I hope you enjoy it. And you will, because you're cool. Thank you for reading.

1

THE VAMPIRE, WHOSE FANGS WERE TOO BIG FOR
his mouth, turned to the camera and hissed.

"Don't look at the camera," said Justin Hollow, the director.

"I keep poking my lip on these things," said Harold, and
he spit the plastic fangs out onto the ground. He hadn't been a
very frightening example of the undead before, and he was even
less scary with no fangs and a thick line of drool running down
his chin.

"Cut!" shouted Justin, loud enough to be sure that the com-
mand was heard by his production crew of two. "C'mon, Harold.
Stay in character. We're three hours behind schedule."

"I don't care. I hate this. You promised that I'd get all the girls
I wanted. So where are all the girls I want?"

Justin let out his thirty-ninth exasperated sigh of the night.
"The movie has to come out first."

"It's not even a real movie."

Justin bristled. It was a full-body bristle, head to toe, which he
hadn't even realized was physically possible. Bobby, who handled
sound recording, and Gabe, who handled everything else, both
stepped back a couple of feet. Neither of them truly believed that

they were about to witness a murder, but they wanted to get out of the splash zone just in case.

Had this been one of Justin's movies, he would have very slowly lowered his camera, stared directly into Harold's eyes with a steely gaze, and then after an extremely dramatic pause, asked, "*What...did...you...just...say?*"

His actual response, delivered in a squeakier voice than he would have allowed from his actors, was, "Huh?"

"I said it's not a real movie." Harold started to wipe the fake blood off his mouth. It didn't come off, and it probably wouldn't for several days. Justin had planned to feel guilty about this later, but now he wouldn't bother. "Nobody's ever going to see it. You probably won't even finish it."

"I finished my last three movies!" Justin insisted. "I got hundreds of hits on YouTube!"

That statement was technically accurate, though it was the lowest possible number of hits you could get and still use "hundred" in its plural form. The only comment anybody posted about his latest film had been, "This twelve-year-old filmmaker sort of shows promise," which really frustrated Justin because he was fifteen.

Harold shrugged. "This is a waste of time. I've got better things to do on a Friday night."

"Nobody ever said this was going to be easy," said Justin, who had indeed said that it was going to be easy when he had lured Harold into the role. "You can quit now, but what are you going to think about your decision ten years from now?"

"I'm going to think, 'Wow, it sure is nice to be such a well-paid dentist.'"

Harold walked off the set. It wasn't an actual set but rather a small park near Justin's home, where they were filming without a permit. Justin knew he should shout something after his ex-actor. Something vicious. Something devastating. He thought about shouting, "You'll never work in this town again!" but no, it had to be something that Harold would consider a *bad* thing.

"Fine!" Justin shouted. "But when we record the audio commentary track for the Blu-ray, I'm going to talk about how you abandoned us, and how much happier everybody was with the new actor who took your role, and how we all agreed that he should have been cast in the first place, and how he had so many girlfriends that he couldn't even keep track of them, and how they all found out about one another and had a great big awesome catfight in his front yard! And I'll pronounce your name wrong!"

Harold continued walking, apparently not heartbroken.

Justin wished he could afford a second camera so that he could smash this one in a rage. An entire evening's worth of shooting, wasted!

"Maybe this is for the best," said Gabe. "We all know he was miscast."

"You're the one who cast him," said Bobby.

"Just so we could use his swimming pool."

"We lost the swimming pool!" Justin wailed. "That's our climax!"

"We can write around this," said Gabe. He stroked his mustache, which could only be seen in direct sunlight, and thought for a moment. "What if the vampire can transform at will? We could get a different actor and still keep all of Harold's scenes. In fact, we could get lots of different actors. We could just replace that person every time somebody quit. A different vampire in each scene! Think about it!"

Justin shook his head. "That won't scare audiences."

"What do you mean? If you were sitting next to somebody, and all of a sudden they turned into a *completely different person*, you'd freak out! You'd be all like, 'Whoa! What happened? That's not how nature works!' If you transformed into Bobby right now, I wouldn't even try to be brave about it. I'd just wet myself and run."

"Can I lower the boom mic now?" asked Bobby.

Justin nodded at Bobby and then shook his head at Gabe. "There's no sense of menace if the vampire is played by eighteen different people."

"Harold had no menace. He could be strangling a koala bear and he wouldn't seem menacing."

"Then why didn't you say something sooner?"

"I did. That one time. And then that other one time. When he tripped during the first take, I said it three different times."

Justin sighed. It was a resigned sigh rather than an exasperated one, so it wasn't part of the official tally. "You're right. You're always right. Let's call it quits for the night and go to Monkey Burger."

Justin held up his cell phone so his mom could clearly see the Monkey Burger logo behind him. Thanks to technology, he could never get away with being someplace he wasn't supposed to be. He hoped that someday this would be inconvenient. He would say, "Oh no! My mom is calling, and I'm at a girl-filled party instead of the library!" But thus far it was merely a disappointing reminder that he never really got into trouble.

"Okay," Mom said. "Have fun!"

Justin assured her that he would and then disconnected the call. He, Gabe, and Bobby went inside the restaurant, which smelled of neither monkeys nor burgers but rather had an aroma sort of like pickles mixed with feet. They went there because it was cheap, close, and open late on weekends, though Justin suspected that the food had been scavenged from the Dumpsters of other restaurants.

They got a large order of chili cheese fries to share and three cups of water. Then they sat down at a booth. Bobby, who had a great appreciation for the act of eating, grabbed the biggest fry off the top and popped it into his mouth.

"Our movies suck," said Justin.

Gabe frowned. He was tall and gawky. He had a permanent cowlick no matter how short he cut his hair, and he looked like he should wear glasses even though his vision was perfectly fine. "What do you mean?"

"I mean, they're awful. We all know it."

"I think you're…" Gabe trailed off and then shrugged. "Okay, you're right. So what do you propose we do?"

"Make a movie that doesn't suck."

"Hey, guys," said Bobby. "These fries are like pressing a lava stick against your tongue, so be careful."

"We're getting better," Gabe insisted. "*Mummy Pit* sucked less than *Werewolf Night*, which sucked less than *Ghost Barn*."

"That's not good enough." Justin picked up one of the fries. The potatoes might have been real, but no actual cow had been involved with the chili or the cheese. In fact, the only resemblance to actual chili and cheese were their colors, brown and yellow(ish) respectively.

"*Vampire Tree* was off to a decent start though," Gabe insisted.

"No, it wasn't."

"That scene with the undead scorpion would've been cool after we added some CGI."

"No, it wouldn't have." Justin ate the fry, which not only failed to burn his mouth but also had somehow already dropped below room temperature. "I don't want to make terrible movies anymore. I want them to be big. I want them to be important. I want them to be longer than ten minutes."

"All right," said Gabe.

"We should change our filmmaking process," said Justin. "We should write a script first."

"I thought you always said that following a script would restrict your creativity on the set and that the best ideas are those that filmmakers generate on the spot."

"I've said a lot of things over the years," said Justin. "This time we need a script. We don't have to stick to it word for word, but we should have one."

"Is there a blister on my tongue?" asked Bobby, sticking out his tongue. "I can't tell if it's a blister or just a piece of fry." Justin and Gabe couldn't understand what he was saying, since his tongue was sticking out, but they'd known him long enough to get the general idea.

"It's a piece of fry," said Justin.

"It won't come off. Why won't it come off?"

"Okay, fine," said Gabe. "We'll have a script."

"And a budget."

"Dude—"

"You can't make the greatest movie ever without a budget," Justin told him.

"Now we're making the greatest movie ever? I thought we were just making one that didn't suck."

"Do you know how old George Romero was when he made *Night of the Living Dead*?"

"Late twenties."

"Right. So we've got a while to catch up. That example didn't really make the point I was trying to make. What I'm saying is that we should be ahead of the curve. We should be making movies that people can't *believe* were made by fifteen-year-olds. I want people to be stunned at what we're making. I want people to accuse us of being genetically enhanced."

"I'm all in favor of that," said Gabe. "I just feel like we should set our sights a little lower. We keep saying we want to make a zombie movie. Maybe instead of the greatest movie ever, we make the greatest *zombie* movie ever."

"The greatest zombie movie ever would, by definition, also be the greatest movie ever."

"Point taken."

"Zombie movie. Good choice, Gabe. And we're going to *commit* ourselves to this project. No safety net. No excuses not to finish. Nobody is going to say this isn't a real movie."

"I really can't get this fry off my tongue," said Bobby. "The cheese is like superglue."

Gabe ignored Bobby and shrugged at Justin. "Okay. So if we're doing a real movie, how do you propose we raise the money?"

Justin stared into Gabe's eyes with a steely gaze, and then after a dramatic pause, he said, "*Any…way…we…can.*"

"Such as?"

"I don't know. Crowdfunding. A bake sale. Insurance fraud. We'll worry about that later."

"I think we should worry about it a little bit now."

"I'm in an ambitious mood. Don't bother me with reality."

Justin picked up a fry and dipped it into the runniest patch of chili. "We can do this. We can make a three-hour epic that will revolutionize the film industry."

"Three hours?"

"At least."

"How about we make half an epic and go for ninety minutes?"

"Actually we should let the story decide for itself how long it needs to be." Justin ate the fry. "Are you in?"

"I don't like that you're giving the story a consciousness of its own."

"Are you in?" Justin pressed.

"I'm in," said Bobby.

"Gabe?"

"I'm going to Indiana for the summer, remember? The day after school gets out."

"Okay, so that gives us a month. We can do it. Are you in?"

"You're insane."

"Are you in?"

"You're also deranged."

"But are you in?"

"You're insane, deranged, and scary."

"So you're in?"

As he had many times during their ten years of friendship, Gabe looked resigned to his fate. "Yeah, I'm in."

Bobby seemed to notice something behind Justin. He smiled. It was a wicked smile, the kind of smile a guy gets when the thoughts in his brain are nothing but the purest evil.

"What?" Justin asked, Bobby's evil aura making him suddenly uncomfortable.

"I know who we should cast in the lead."

"Who?"

Bobby pointed to a booth at the other end of the restaurant. "Alicia Howtz."

2

"NO," SAID JUSTIN.

"Why not?" asked Bobby.

"She isn't right for the role."

"We don't have a role yet."

"She won't be right when we do have one."

"Could it be because, I don't know, let me think, gosh, you're madly in love with her?"

It was indeed because Justin was madly in love with Alicia. Okay, *moderately* in love with her. He had been for the past four years. During those four years, they'd had exactly three conversations consisting of a total of eleven sentences, the content of which was yes, Justin did know what time it was, no, Justin did not have change for a five, and, in their most recent exchange, "Excuse me."

They had never shared any classes. Their lockers were on opposite ends of the school. They didn't ride the same bus. In fact, he could go weeks without seeing her.

Without seeing her beautiful, long blond hair…

Without seeing her beautiful blue eyes…

Without seeing her beautiful smile…

(He'd fallen in love with her when she wore braces, and he had found her smile to be entrancing even then. Now it was absolutely radiant.)

Her body was like a goddess mixed with an angel mixed with a female superhero.

Justin knew that he didn't stand a chance with her, which is why he never tried to stand a chance with her. He didn't look like Gollum or anything, but he also wouldn't ever cast himself as the lead in one of his movies.

She was gorgeous. He was a film geek.

"No," said Justin. He was lying though. It really was because he was madly in love with her.

"This could be your chance," said Bobby. "If you cast her in the movie, she'd think of you as her director. Girls love directors. You'd stop just being that guy she sees in her peripheral vision every once in a while."

"We don't know if she can act."

"So we'll write lines where she doesn't have to act much."

"I'm all in favor of Justin getting together with Alicia," said Gabe, "but this isn't how you go about the casting process."

Bobby slid out of the booth and stood up. "I'm going to offer her a part."

Justin had a sudden moment of panic. "What? No. Don't."

"You said you wanted to do this without a safety net, right? Without any excuses not to finish? Then cast Alicia."

Justin had to admit that offering Alicia the lead in his movie *would* give him the motivation to get it done, but his idea of committing himself to the film had involved "risking and perhaps losing enormous sums of somebody else's money" and not "risking Alicia Howtz thinking he was a complete loser."

"We should wait," said Justin.

"If we wait, we might wake up tomorrow and decide that this was a terrible idea."

"Exactly! That's why we should wait!"

"But then you'll wake up tomorrow and not be making a movie with Alicia Howtz as the star." Bobby took a step toward Alicia's booth, where she sat with four or five friends Justin didn't know. "Are you coming?"

"If you do this, I will kill you," said Justin.

"Don't do it," Gabe told Bobby. "I won't help him kill you, but I'll be really mad. We'll write the part with an eye toward casting her in the lead, and if she passes the audition process, then we'll offer her the role. And if she accepts, then Justin is more than welcome to be the kind of sleazy director who would hit on his lead actress."

"I wouldn't hit on her," said Justin. "I would maybe—*maybe*—be open to forming a friendship during our time together on the set. We can see where it leads at the end of the shooting schedule after our professional relationship is over."

"Look how much you're sweating," said Bobby.

"I promise we'll try to get her involved in the movie," Justin said. "Just wait for us to have a title first."

Bobby slid back into the booth. "Okay, but I'm not going to let you wuss out on this."

"Fine."

Justin wiped the perspiration from his brow. No doubt it was from the chili and not the terror.

As Justin lay in bed, too wired to fall asleep, he wondered if his idea had perhaps been just a tiny little bit overly ambitious.

Nah, he decided.

Maybe they'd fail. Maybe they'd only make the third or fourth greatest zombie movie of all time. That was okay. There was no shame in that.

One month—actually, twenty-nine days—was not a lot of time to write a script and shoot an entire movie, especially since they had school and part-time jobs and curfews. But when Justin set his mind to something, whether it was getting one hundred percent on a chemistry test or watching forty-eight hours' worth of horror movies in a row, he always succeeded.

Okay, that wasn't completely true. When he was eleven, he'd set his mind to being the ultimate Hollywood stuntman, and four years after the cast came off, he still couldn't lift his right arm all the way. Last year he had set his mind to stop being afraid of the neighbor's pit bull and to befriend the animal instead. That hadn't worked out in the best possible manner either.

In fact, now that he was thinking about it, there had been many, many, many instances in which he'd put his mind to something and the end result had been pain, humiliation, or a combination of the two. But Justin was fine with that. Pain was temporary. On his third movie, he'd been conked on the forehead by a baseball bat that had slipped out of his lead actor's hand during an intense "bash the mummy with a baseball bat" sequence, and the pain had gone away after only two days.

Perhaps brain damage was forever, but pain was temporary.

And humiliation? Justin didn't purposely invite humiliation into his life, but unless it involved the potential for having his heart crushed by girls, he thought of most incidents in terms of how good of an anecdote they'd provide for talk show interviews. It was fine to look stupid on occasion. Nobody liked people who were popular all the time.

He really needed to get some sleep, so he tried counting zombie heads. When he counted his five hundredth zombie head, he settled for planning out his Oscar speech.

He wasn't going to be one of those people who rattled off a list of names, thanking studio executives who could help their careers. He'd thank Gabe and Bobby, of course, and his parents, and the girlfriend he would definitely have at the time, which would almost certainly not be Alicia; however, he saw no need to eliminate her from this particular fantasy.

He'd start with a killer joke. He hoped something would happen during the ceremony that would give him an idea for a hilarious ad-lib. But he'd have a planned bit ready just to be completely prepared.

Maybe he'd say, "I never expected to win!" but read it directly off a piece of paper. He'd read it slowly in a monotone voice so that the audience got the joke. Then he'd do the ad-lib that would delight both the live audience and the millions of viewers at home, thank people in a heartwarming manner, and then say something inspirational, all before his time ended and the band played him off. It wouldn't be generic inspiration like, "Kids, follow your heart and your dreams will come true!" It would be inspiring yet also practical advice. There wasn't a lot of practical advice in Academy Awards acceptance speeches, so he'd get a lot of positive press for that along with his hilarious ad-lib.

Even as the applause filled his imagination, Justin knew that his chances of winning an Oscar for his zombie movie were slim at best. He probably wouldn't tell Gabe or Bobby that he was planning his acceptance speech.

His alarm—the cruel, rotten, traitorous, heartless, demonic piece of junk—went off at 6:00 a.m., as it did every Saturday. Justin got up, scratched in seven or eight places, and then stumbled into the bathroom to take a shower, wishing he could just curl up in the bathtub and go back to sleep.

But he couldn't be late to work, or Mr. Pamm would yell at him even more than he did when he *wasn't* mad. Mr. Pamm loved to shout. He didn't shout to deliver constructive criticism or even to express disapproval of bad behavior. Mostly he yelled about purely hypothetical situations, such as, *"Dang it, Justin. If you drop that dang box of apples, it's coming out of your dang paycheck!"* or, *"Mop that dang floor before somebody dang falls. Dang it!"* Obviously a freshly mopped floor was a greater danger for falling than one that merely had some dirty footprints on it, but questioning Mr. Pamm's logic was unwise.

Working at the craft store warehouse was a terrible job. (The aforementioned apples were decorative plastic ones.) But at least it was better than washing dishes, cleaning fish, swinging a pickax in a coal mine, digging ditches, unclogging toilets that had been clogged weeks ago, testing the acidic effects of mascara on human flesh, being punched by a sadistic millionaire who paid people to let him punch them, or working airline customer service.

And unlike Gabe's job, which required him to think about how much whipped cream to put on the sundae, or Bobby's job, which required him to prioritize which groceries were best suited for the bottom of the bag and which were best suited for the top, Justin's job required very little brainpower wattage. When he wasn't actively being yelled at, he could think about pretty much anything he wanted.

So at 7:15 a.m., as he unloaded boxes from a truck, he thought about his zombie movie.

How deeply should he really commit himself to this idea?

It would be very easy to keep the stakes low. Not make a big deal out of it. Tinker with a screenplay and see what happened. Despite peer pressure from Bobby, Justin was the director, so he didn't *have* to cast Alicia if he decided that his nervous system couldn't handle it.

And if they failed, they could have the following conversation:

"Whoops," Justin would say. "Apparently we did not make the greatest zombie movie ever after all."

"Nope," Gabe would say, shaking his head but not in a vigorous manner. "We didn't even finish it, film any scenes, cast any actors, or even write anything. But that's all right, because we kept the stakes low!"

"It's fun to fail when there's no accountability!" Bobby would say.

That wasn't acceptable.

To make sure he finished this project, Justin had to set up legitimate stakes. He needed to tell everybody he could about the movie. Create so much buzz that people would *demand* to know when it was coming out. Make it so he'd have to scream, "Leave me alone! Leave me alone! Quit bugging me about the zombie movie! Let me live my life in peace!" if he failed to deliver.

He'd post it everywhere online. Make a quick teaser trailer.

Create posters. Let the world know that something incredible was on the way.

Mr. Pamm noisily told him not to drop a box that he'd been nowhere close to dropping.

Mr. Pamm. That would be the perfect name for the first person to get eaten by zombies.

The first official preproduction meeting took place that afternoon in Justin's bedroom. As Gabe and Bobby dined on chicken salad sandwiches that were provided by craft services (Justin's mom), Justin flipped to a blank page of his easel pad, took the cap off a red Magic Marker, and wrote, *Greatest zombie movie ever.*

"You should make the words look like they're bleeding," said Bobby.

"No," said Justin. "That's the first thing we all need to understand. This isn't going to be the kind of movie where the title is in bleeding letters. We're not doing a cheesy zombie flick. This is going to be true horror."

"Awesome," said Bobby.

"And we're going to get this movie done, no matter what."

"You're pretty passionate about a project with no title, characters, or story," Gabe noted.

"Yes, I am. Now after giving it some consideration, I've decided that Gabe is right about the three-hour running time not being such a great idea. But that doesn't mean we're going to reduce our scope. This is going to be epic." He wrote *EPIC* on the pad. "If anybody in this room does not feel that they can deliver on this word," he said, tapping the word *EPIC*, "then they should get out now."

Neither Gabe nor Bobby left the room, though they didn't let out mighty roars of assent either.

"This is our first meeting, not counting last night, which wasn't a real meeting, so it's just for brainstorming. This is a safe, judgment-free time for sharing. Remember, there are no stupid ideas."

"The zombies should live in piñatas," said Bobby.

Justin glared at him. "Is this how you're going to act?"

"You said—"

"I know what I said, and you know what I meant. This is a real thing, and we need to take it seriously."

Bobby nodded. "I withdraw my piñata idea."

"Thank you."

Gabe raised his hand.

"Yes, Gabe?"

"We don't have any money."

"That's why we have to be inventive. Did the makers of *The Blair Witch Project* have any money?"

"Yes, they had twenty thousand dollars. We don't have twenty thousand dollars."

"We don't need it."

"And that's a low estimate of how much they spent. They spent way more after the shooting was done."

"Right, but that was studio money after they got a distribution deal. All we care about right now is the cost of shooting the movie."

"We don't have twenty thousand dollars," said Gabe.

"No, but do you know what we do have?"

"Twenty dollars?"

Justin scowled. "Why are you being so negative?"

"I'm the producer. My job is to be practical."

"Compromise my creative vision in our second meeting, okay?"

"Will do."

Justin cleared his throat and tapped the word *EPIC* again. "We can do this. And while I was at work, I came up with the perfect title." He wrote *Lifeless* on the pad.

"*Lifeless?*" Bobby asked.

"Right. Without life. Dead. The perfect name for a zombie movie."

"I don't know," said Gabe. "I can see a critic saying, '*Lifeless* is an accurate title for this lifeless film.'"

Justin crossed out *Lifeless*. "Other ideas?"

"*Dead Zombies*," said Bobby.

"Zombies are already dead."

"These are even deader."

Justin reluctantly wrote *Dead Zombies* on the board.

"Hmmmm," said Gabe. "How about *Zombie Night*. No, *Dead Night*. No, *The Dead in Florida*. *The Florida Dead*. *Florida Zombies*. *Florizombies*. Maybe something about humidity. *Hurricane Zombies*. *Zombie Hurricane*. *Zombie Tornado*. *Zombie Volcano*. *Zombie Earthquake*. *Earthquake of the Zombies*. *Earthquake of the Dead*. *The Earth Quakes When the Dead Rise*. *DeadQuake*. Maybe something about flesh eating. *Dining on Flesh*. *The Dead Dine on Flesh*. *Dead Flesh Diners*. You're not writing these down."

"You're going too fast."

"I like *Florizombies*," said Bobby.

"What was the one after *Zombie Night?*" asked Justin.

After a couple of minutes, they recreated the list of titles and added a few more, including *Zombies with Flesh Stuck in Their Teeth*, even though Justin was insistent that this would not be a zombie comedy.

Bobby's cell phone rang. He took it out of his pocket, looked at the display, and then hurriedly put it away again.

"Who's calling you?" Justin asked.

"Nobody."

"I saw it," said Gabe. "It's Alicia."

"You called Alicia?"

Bobby pressed his hand against his pocket as his phone continued to ring as if muffling the noise would make Justin ask fewer questions.

"You seriously called Alicia?" Justin asked.

"No! I texted her! I didn't know she'd call! Should I answer it?"

"No!" said Justin.

Bobby took the phone out of his pocket. "I should answer. She might never call back. I'll put her on speaker."

"No! Don't put her on speaker!"

Bobby touched the screen of his phone. "Hello?" he said.

"Is this Bobby?" asked the beautiful and melodic yet frightening voice of Alicia Howtz.

3

"YES, THIS IS ROBERT GREEN," SAID BOBBY. "I'M so glad you called to discuss this professional opportunity. We're currently in the midst of a preproduction meeting, so your timing is perfect."

Justin gestured frantically at him. *Put her on mute*, he mouthed at Bobby.

Bobby gave him a quizzical look.

Justin pointed at the phone. *Put her on mute, or I will grab you by the ears and bash your head into the floor.* He mimed the ear-grabbing and head-bashing as he said it.

"I'm sorry, Alicia, but our director insists on speaking with you directly. Please note that by speaking to him about the project, you are verbally signing a nondisclosure agreement. Is that acceptable?"

"Uh, sure," said Alicia.

"Excellent." Bobby handed the phone to Justin.

Justin stared at the phone for a moment as if it were a python about to strike.

"Hello?" said Alicia.

Justin continued to stare at the phone as if it were a great white shark about to bite him in half, lengthwise.

"Are you on mute?" Alicia asked.

Justin kept staring at the phone as if it were a genetically engineered hybrid of a lion, a piranha, and a tarantula.

Gabe gave him a look that said, *I disagree with the tactic our friend just used, but now that he's done it, you might as well talk to her.*

Bobby replied with a look that said, *Talk, dork!*

"Hello, Alicia," said Justin. "This is Justin Hollow. We've seen each other around school and talked a couple of times." He didn't tell her that it was eleven sentences because the fact that he knew the exact number might seem creepy.

"Yep, I know who you are."

"Oh, good, that saves time. Anyway, I wanted to offer you the lead role in my new movie."

Bobby seemed much happier about Justin blurting out this offer than Gabe did, so Justin decided to only look at Bobby for the remainder of the phone call.

"What's the movie?"

"It's a zombie movie."

"Okay."

Was that a pro-zombie-movie okay or an anti-zombie-movie okay? Justin couldn't tell.

"It'll be a feature film. Probably not three hours but way more than ten minutes."

"What's it called?"

"We don't have a final title yet. The working title is *Zombies with Flesh Stuck in Their Teeth.*" Justin could tell that Gabe was frantically shaking his head, but he focused his attention on Bobby's nose.

"It's a comedy?"

"No, that's just a temporary title. Doesn't really reflect the movie. We may or may not have any shots of flesh stuck in a zombie's teeth. That may not even be the final temporary title. This is all still in the early stages."

"Okay. So what's the character like?"

"Well, her name is"—*Think! Think!*—"Veronica Chaos, and she's in a postapocalyptic world"—Gabe's shaking head was a blur of motion in the corner of his eye—"with mutant zombies everywhere"—Gabe smacked him on the shoulder—"and she has to find the lost"—*Medallion? Skull? Child?*—"book that can save humanity. She carries a"—*Sword? Chainsaw? Lightweight lawn mower?*—"cat and wears a"—*Cloak? Corset? Chain mail bikini?*—"tattered white wedding dress."

"That sounds pretty cool," said Alicia.

"Oh yeah. It's going to make *Return of the Living Dead* look like *Return of the Living Dead, Part 5.*"

"Is it going to play in theaters?"

"Of course. Maybe not in the summer but definitely a wide release."

Gabe got up and walked out of the room.

"When does it start filming?"

"The shooting schedule is still being put together. We're working on the final polish of the script, and I'll have it to you on Monday."

"Well, this sounds great, Justin! I'd love to be in your movie!"

"I'm very pleased to hear that," said Justin. "My people will draw up the contract and get it to you ASAP."

"Thanks! I'll see you at school."

"Good-bye."

Justin disconnected the call.

He and Bobby stared at each other for a while.

"Okay," said Justin. "I probably shouldn't have told her that we were going to get a wide theatrical release."

"Probably not."

"Aside from that, it went fine, right?"

Bobby shrugged. "She took the part."

"Yep. We've got our lead. That's one big hurdle out of the way. How mad is Gabe?"

"His face was pretty red."

"But his face is red a lot of the time. That doesn't necessarily mean anything. He can't help his complexion."

"Nope."

"Hey, Gabe?" Justin called out.

Gabe walked back into Justin's bedroom. His face was still quite red.

"We've got our lead actress," said Justin. "So that's, y'know, one less thing you'll need to worry about. We're well on our way."

"Our working title is not *Zombies with Skin Stuck in Their Teeth.*"

"It's flesh, not sk… Actually I'm not going to correct you. You're right. But what was I supposed to do? I didn't call her! Bobby shoved the phone in my hand! He's the one your face should be so red about!"

"I'm mad at Bobby too."

"Why are you mad at *me?*" asked Bobby.

"Because you texted Alicia about the movie without clearing it with either of us! This is your fault!"

"But that's the only thing you're mad about, right?"

"Right."

Bobby smiled. "I can live with that."

"Don't do it again," said Gabe. "We can't have crew members going rogue. But we're not going to talk about that anymore.

We're going to talk about the greatest zombie movie ever, which apparently is going to get a wide theatrical release and feature Veronica Chaos."

"Not a bad name off the top of my head, huh?"

"Be serious."

"I am serious. I just…" Justin trailed off as the realization of what he'd done trampled over him like a mechanical rhinoceros. "I…I…I…I…I…I…I…"

"Go on," Gabe prodded.

Justin lifted his shirt to wipe the perspiration off his forehead. What had he been thinking? They didn't have a script or time or money, and he'd promised Alicia that she'd see herself up on the big screen. She was going to find out that he was a total fraud. Girls of her level of quality weren't attracted to total frauds.

"I think I'm going to throw up," said Justin.

"Go ahead," said Gabe. "It's your room."

Justin mopped up more sweat. "Okay. So. Um. Yeah. I wanted to be fully committed to the project, and now I am. If we fail, none of us will have a girlfriend until we move to a new town, so this is exactly what we wanted, right?"

"I'm not sure it is," said Gabe.

Justin said, "We have twenty-eight days to shoot this movie. Twenty-seven if you don't count today. But we'll count today, so twenty-eight. Lots of people have made movies in twenty-eight days. It'll be fun."

"I'm in," said Gabe. "Completely in. I want to make that clear because I'm about to say a bunch of negative things."

"All right. Let's hear them."

Gabe stood up and walked over to the Tampa Bay Buccaneers calendar that was on the wall. Justin didn't like football or any other sports. But his dad had bought him the calendar, and displaying it was a small price to pay to make Dad happy.

"We have twenty-eight days before I leave," said Gabe. "But only three weekends, if you don't count this weekend."

"Let's count this weekend."

"Fine. Three and a half weekends. So technically we only have seven full days. We're not skipping school to make this movie."

"I never would have suggested such a thing," said Justin.

"That doesn't count work. I don't know my schedule yet, but I'll probably have to work two or three of those seven days. Bobby works Tuesdays and Thursdays. You work Thursdays and Saturdays. What are we going to do about that?"

"I've thought about that," said Justin, even though he really hadn't, "and I figured we could call in sick."

"For a full month?"

"Not every day of the month necessarily."

"What happens when they find out we were making a movie?"

"Then they'll know it was a noble cause."

"No way will my mom let me call in sick," said Bobby.

"Does she have to know about it?"

"If we're trying to make a giant epic spectacle, then yeah, the news will probably get back to her."

"And also you're forgetting one big thing," said Gabe.

"What?"

"Finals week."

"Okay. Yes, that's a pretty big thing. We'll work around it."

"We have to study."

"I know. I'm not saying that we have to flunk our exams for our art. We'll figure it out."

Justin went over to the easel, turned over a new page on the pad, and wrote *Things to Worry about Later* at the top. Under that, he wrote *Schedule*.

"What about money?" Gabe asked.

Justin wrote *Money* underneath *Schedule*.

Gabe shook his head. "As the producer, I say we stress about money now."

"We're going to keep this cost-effective. We've already got the camera. Cast and crew will work for a screen credit obviously. We'll use locations that we can get for free like the school. We take it for granted, but our school has tons of production value. What about product placement? If we show the Monkey Burger logo up close, they might give us free food."

"Would they want their restaurant featured in a movie called *Zombies with Flesh Stuck in Their Teeth*?" asked Bobby.

"That's not the name of the movie! That was never going to be the name of the movie! For now, let's call it *Untitled Epic Zombie Movie*. Does that work for everybody?"

"If this is just a temporary title, how about *The Greatest Zombie Movie Ever*?"

"No, that sounds egotistical."

"UEZM isn't a very good acronym," said Bobby.

"Then don't acronym it. We're getting sidetracked."

"Right," said Gabe. "Let's get back to money."

"If we can get free food, then really we wouldn't have to pay for much except makeup and explosives."

"We need machine guns," said Bobby.

"Right, right," said Justin. He looked at Gabe. "*Prop* machine guns, Mr. Oh No, We're Gonna Accidentally Kill Somebody."

"I knew that you meant props."

"If it were up to me, we'd do all old-school practical effects, but that's not realistic at our current budget level of zero. So our rule is no CGI blood, but helicopter crashes and giant cracks in the earth and stuff will be computer-generated. Everybody okay with that?"

Gabe and Bobby nodded.

"Good. Now we just need a story."

4

JUSTIN STARED AT THE SCREEN OF HIS LAPTOP.
Eight in the morning came pretty quickly when you were up until four thirty brainstorming ideas, and he'd almost hit the wonderful, wonderful snooze button…but no. He had a lot of writing to do today. It was time to use the skills he'd perfected over all these years of waiting until the night before to write essays.

They'd divided the story into three parts. Justin had wanted to write the third part, which had the most carnage, but they drew straws (well, pretzel sticks) to decide who got to write what. Gabe got the second part, and Bobby got the third. They'd both spent the night at his house and were asleep on the floor. He'd tried to rouse Gabe, but then he was politely told to die. He knew better than to try to poke Bobby. That was a good way to lose a finger. They'd just have to write faster to catch up.

He continued to stare at the screen. *Look how blank I am!*, the screen seemed to say.

Maybe he'd write better if he got some more sleep.

No. Sleep was a luxury he could not afford if he was going to achieve his goal. Sleep was for losers who *weren't* trying to make the greatest zombie movie ever. Maybe he'd have permanent dark circles under his eyes. Maybe he'd start hallucinating bloodthirsty orangutans, and maybe he'd become so delirious that he'd forget how to blink. But those were the sacrifices of a true artist.

Then again Alicia might like him better if he didn't spend all day twitching and babbling incoherently.

He'd worry about his never-gonna-happen relationship with Alicia later. For now he had to focus entirely on the movie. It was time to write.

FADE IN:

INT. CITY STREET – NIGHT

A helicopter crashes to the ground, crushing dozens of zombies. It rolls down the street, leaving a thick smear of squished zombies in its path, until it finally hits a tall building, which crashes to the ground.

As the cloud of dust clears, we hear only the sound of zombies moaning. They're everywhere. The apocalypse has not been kind to this city.

But then, impossibly, the helicopter door opens! VERONICA CHAOS, 15 and stunningly beautiful even with all of the lacerations covering her body, crawls out, wearing a shredded white wedding dress. She's holding a cat.

She gazes up at the sky and howls in primal anguish.

The TITLE appears on-screen: UNTITLED ZOMBIE MOVIE.

[*Note to self: Add real title when we know it.*]

Perfect! This could not be flowing any better. At this rate he'd be done with his third of the script by lunchtime. In fact, it was going so well that he could get in a quick game of—

No! No games. Famous filmmakers didn't have time for video games. If you showed up at Peter Jackson's house, he wouldn't be sitting there playing *Minecraft*. The only thing he had time for was to check Reddit and—

No! No Reddit. He needed to remain completely focused on this script until he'd written his thirty to thirty-three pages. Especially since he might have to pick up some of Gabe's and/or Bobby's slack. Bathroom breaks were acceptable if they weren't too frequent, but aside from that, Justin needed to maintain laser focus. Cyborg focus. Nothing existed in his world except for this screenplay.

Veronica walks down the street, limping a bit because she was just in a helicopter crash. A pair of zombies runs toward her.

"Fast zombies or slow zombies?" Justin had asked last night, early in the story development discussion.

"Slow zombies," said Gabe.

"Fast zombies," said Bobby.

"Slow zombies are scarier."

"No, they're not. Fast zombies are scarier because they're fast."

"Fast zombies aren't realistic."

"*Zombies* aren't realistic."

"If you were a corpse that came back to life, you wouldn't be moving fast," Gabe insisted. "It doesn't make any sense. Decomposed muscles are slow."

"You can just walk away from slow zombies," said Bobby. "Just la-di-da, strolling along. Oops, that one is kind of close. I'd better veer slightly to the left. Uh-oh, there's another one. I suppose I'll have to shove it over."

"Until you're overwhelmed by their sheer numbers," said Gabe. "That's the whole point of zombies. They don't seem like a huge threat until suddenly you're surrounded and there's no way to escape. You're doomed."

"You're more doomed if you're surrounded by fast zombies."

"*Shaun of the Dead* has slow zombies."

"*Zombieland* has fast zombies."

"Lucio Fulci's *Zombie* has slow zombies."

"*28 Days Later* has fast."

"Those aren't zombies. Those are the infected."

"They're zombies."

"They're the infected."

"Stop being such a zombie snob."

"I'm not being a snob. I'm being accurate."

"*Dawn of the Dead* has fast zombies."

"No, *Dawn of the Dead* has slow zombies."

"It has fast zombies," said Bobby. "I watched it last week. We'll put in the Blu-ray."

"Which one are you talking about?"

"*Dawn of the Dead.*"

"No, which version?"

"I'm talking about the remake."

"Well, I'm talking about the original."

"The remake was better."

"Get out of my house," said Gabe. "I mean Justin's house."

"I'm allowed to express my opinion. You can't tell me that if you were walking down the sidewalk and somebody said, 'Hey, dude, I'm going to release a dozen zombies to chase after you. Would you prefer that I release the fast-moving variety or the slow-moving variety?' you wouldn't request the slow-moving ones."

"That's real life. This is a movie."

"You're the one who was talking about realism."

"Okay," said Gabe. "If we're going to try to make the greatest zombie movie ever, then we need to pay homage to the original classic, *Night of the Living Dead*. Therefore, we need to go with slow zombies. Case closed."

"The first zombie in *Night of the Living Dead* chased after Barbara in her car, so technically it had both fast *and* slow zombies. Ha! Logic fail!"

"That's it!" said Justin. "We'll have the best of both worlds. Our movie will have both fast and slow zombies. Guaranteed mass appeal!"

"What about talking zombies?" asked Bobby.

"No talking zombies," said Justin and Gabe, almost simultaneously.

"*Return of the Living Dead* had talking zombies."

"Shut up," Justin and Gabe said.

Veronica watches the zombies, her expression unreadable. But then she…smiles.

VERONICA
Sorry, guys. Not today.

She takes out a machine gun [*Note to self: Fig-*
ure out where she was keeping the machine gun.]
and opens fire. The zombies' heads turn to goopy
mush, and they drop to the ground. [*Note to*
self: It would be cool if the mush formed the
shape of something that symbolizes our movie's
theme.] [*Note to self: Discuss theme with Gabe*
and Bobby.]

More zombies begin to run toward her! She puts
the cat on her shoulder and takes out a second
machine gun.

VERONICA
You wanna play, huh? Consider
it playtime.

With a machine gun in each hand, Veronica pulls the
triggers and spins in a circle, mowing down zombies
like crazy. She's like a zombie-slaying ballerina.

Justin wondered what the record was for the most zombies
killed in a single movie. Maybe he'd try to break that record in the
opening *scene*.

Well, no, the story had to come first. If his plot naturally lent
itself to setting the world record for the most zombies ever splat-
tered in a single movie, he'd go that route.

Bobby rolled over onto his back and began to snore. When he snored, it sounded like he was choking to death on his own tongue. Usually Justin was able to ignore it, but not while he was trying to be a genius. "Hey, Bobby," he said. "Roll over."

"*Not enough butter on my Pop-Tart,*" said Bobby, not waking up. He resumed his snoring.

"Roll over, Bobby."

"*That cow doesn't really have hair. It's a toupee.*"

Gabe sat up and rubbed his eyes. "Is he dreaming?"

"I hope so."

Bobby let out a snore so otherworldly that no sound designer could recreate it for a motion picture. Then he rolled back over on his side.

Gabe got out of his sleeping bag and looked over Justin's shoulder. "I see that you've started our no-budget film with a helicopter crash."

"Yes."

Gabe shrugged. "All right. We'll figure it out."

A few minutes later, Justin's mom peeked into his room to ask if they were ready for breakfast. Justin decided that food was probably a good idea if he wanted to keep himself alive during the writing process, so he and Gabe headed downstairs, letting Bobby sleep.

They sat at the dining room table, where his mom had set out scrambled eggs, hash browns, bacon, pancakes, and toast. "Where's Bobby?" she asked.

"Still asleep."

"But blueberry pancakes are his favorite."

His mom really liked Bobby and Gabe, calling them her "bonus sons." Justin's dad liked them too, although Justin suspected that he kept an invoice of food costs that he wanted to present to their parents. Bobby lived with his mom, three little sisters (Becky, Bonnie, and Betty), and five dogs (Bongo, Boink, Bleeper, Booga, and Bippity). Since Justin was allergic to dogs, he never went over there. Gabe, like Justin, was an only child, but his mom and dad were strong believers in a clothing-optional lifestyle, so Justin's parents didn't really like him to go over there. Neither did Gabe.

"So what are your plans for today?" Mom asked.

"We're writing the script for a zombie movie. Our first feature."

"Is it going to be R-rated?"

Justin chuckled. "At least."

"I wish you wouldn't watch R-rated movies."

"We're not watching one. We're making one."

Justin's mom was an overprotective parent in a lot of ways, but she didn't restrict his movie watching as long as he continued to demonstrate that he could tell the difference between fantasy and reality. Though she was not a fan of his enthusiasm for horror movies, she knew there were much worse things he could be doing with his friends, like vandalism or treason.

"Keep those grades up, and you can watch as many eyeballs getting poked out as you want," Dad often told him, when the subject came up. "The first time those grades drop, no more severed heads for you."

"What's it about?" Mom asked.

"A survivor in a postapocalyptic landscape. The whole city is overrun by the living dead. To stay alive, she has to rely on her wits and her machine guns."

"Well, it's nice that you have a female lead. Hopefully she'll be a good role model. But why don't you try making a *nice* movie sometime?"

"We might. Someday."

"People like nice movies. You could make a movie that makes people feel better about the world around them. Why don't you make a movie about an immigrant who overcomes adversity?"

"Zombies are adversity."

"Or make a movie about a kid with a disease who ends up not dying from it. Something that inspires people. What's that one movie? The one that makes everybody happy. The one with that one girl. Ron, you know which one I mean, right?"

"*The Wizard of Oz?*"

"No."

"*Paul Blart: Mall Cop 2?*"

"No."

"*The Hobbit: Battle of the Five Armies?*"

"No."

"*The Exorcist?*" asked Justin.

"Don't be a wise guy. You both know which movie I'm talking about."

"We really don't."

"It'll come to me in the middle of the night. Anyway, you should consider making something that critics will call the feel-good movie of the year."

Justin grinned. "I could film ninety minutes of two people making out."

"Very funny."

"I could cast myself as the lead."

"If you don't want to use my suggestions, that's fine. I just think people enjoy movies where they leave with a song in their heart." Mom's eyes lit up. "You could do a musical!"

"A zombie musical?"

"No, a real musical! Like that one movie."

"*The Exorcist*?"

"Stop it. Would you like some more bacon, Gabe?"

"Yes, ma'am."

Justin's mom put two more slices of bacon on Gabe's plate. "Think about what I've said. The world loves movies that aren't rated R."

"Don't worry," said Justin. "I'll do a G-rated version just for you." *A thirty-five-second version*, he thought.

"Thank you."

"By the way, Dad, can I borrow twenty thousand dollars?"

"Nope."

"You sure?"

"Pretty sure."

"Okay."

"On a serious note though, if you really are looking for financing, you should consider talking to Grandma."

"Really?"

Dad nodded. "She's not going to give you twenty grand, but if you need money for supplies, I bet she'd be willing to pitch in."

This was surprising news to Justin. Grandma always included a ten-dollar bill in her birthday cards, but she'd reacted to his three short films by informing him that they were "cute, dear." He'd never considered her as a source of funding.

"Maybe I should call her," he said.

"If I were you, I'd go over there this afternoon. She's always in a good mood right after Sunday brunch, and her mood gets worse the longer it is since she's eaten Sunday brunch."

"We will." Today was supposed to be an all-writing

extravaganza, but he'd happily adjust the schedule to accommodate potential investors.

"Tell Grandma it's a feel-good musical," said Mom.

5

GRANDMA LIVED A HALF AN HOUR AWAY BY BICYCLE in a nice gated community. Justin, Gabe, and Bobby sat on her couch, eating Grandma's special chocolate-chip cookies, which tasted delicious but had the texture of saltwater taffy. Her lemonade was so sour that it made your mouth twist into a vortex. Almost everything in her house was light blue, and Justin had purposely changed into a light-blue shirt to go better with the décor and perhaps make her more inclined to part with her cash.

Grandma sat across from them on her piano bench. She was a plump, gray-haired woman who'd moved to Florida after Grandpa died last year. She took a bite of cookie and chewed it slowly, thoughtfully.

"How much do you need?" she asked.

"Pretty much whatever you're willing to give us."

"That's kind of vague. Don't Hollywood movies cost two hundred million dollars these days?"

Justin nodded. "That's why we're going the independent route."

"How much would it cost me to get Daniel Day-Lewis in your movie?"

"Um, I'm not sure. A lot, I think."

Grandma took another bite of her cookie and then flicked the rest at Justin, hitting him in the forehead. "Daniel Day-Lewis isn't going to be in your zombie movie. Don't be ridiculous. If you think that an acclaimed actor like him is going to show up and star in a movie made by a fifteen-year-old, then you don't understand the film business."

"I didn't actually think that he was going to be in my movie," said Justin. "I was just sort of…you know—"

"Humoring me?"

"Yeah."

"Humoring an old lady. Making her think that she can meet Daniel Day-Lewis. You've gone Hollywood already, kid. You'll say anything to anybody, even your own grandmother, to get what you want."

Justin glanced nervously at Gabe, who avoided his glance.

Grandma laughed. "Relax! I'm just kidding. Jeez, you're uptight. What has your dad been feeding you? Poodle food?" She took a long swig of her lemonade and licked her lips. "Mmmm, mmmm, mmmm. Tangy. So you have a completed script, right?"

"We're working on it today," said Justin.

"How many other investors have you lined up?"

"None. Just you."

"So that means I get final script approval, right?"

Justin stiffened, then forced himself to shrug. "Sure, I guess."

Grandma laughed. "Chillax, Justin. Chillax! I'm not really seeking final script approval. You don't give up script approval to anybody who waves a couple of bucks in your face. I don't even want to read it. That zombie stuff gives me nightmares. As far as I'm concerned, when you die, you should stay dead. All of that rising from the grave and walking around and biting nice people on the arm…it's rude is what it is. Flat-out inconsiderate."

"We should call our movie *Night of the Impolite Dead*," said Bobby.

"Here's what I'm going to do," said Grandma. "I believe in you, so I'm going to take out a second mortgage on my home, sell my wedding ring, and empty my savings."

Justin's eyes widened. "What? No. Don't do that."

Grandma's whole body shook as she cackled with laughter. "I was just seeing if you were the kind of grandson who would let his Grandma risk losing her home."

"Did you think I *might* be?"

"Nah. I just liked seeing your face. It's a good face. Okay, enough fun and games. You're here for a business transaction, and I won't torture you any longer. I'm not a rich woman, but I've socked away a little over the years. And I'm prepared to give you five thousand dollars."

"Seriously?"

"Seriously."

"Grandma, that's…that's fantastic! We can buy hundreds of gallons of fake blood with that!" Justin couldn't believe it. Five thousand dollars! It wasn't enough to pay for the hummus budget on a big summer blockbuster, but he, Gabe, and Bobby could get an incredible amount of production value for that much money.

"Now I'm looking at this as an investment. I'm going to see a return on my investment, right?"

"Oh yeah, sure, sure, absolutely."

Grandma's eyes went cold, and she was no longer smiling. "I said…I'm going to see a return on my investment, *right*?"

Justin couldn't tell if she was kidding again.

"Well, yeah, I mean, these things are never guaranteed, but—"

"I've been joking around a lot during our meeting today," said Grandma. "It's what I do. I like to be the jolly old grandmother. 'Oh, she's a hoot!' people say. But I'm not being a hoot right now. Right now I am being deeply serious. If I give you this money, it is not a birthday gift. It is not money for you to go out for ice cream with your friends. When I write you this check for five thousand dollars, I expect you to write me a check for *more* than five thousand dollars after this movie is released. I expect at *least* a twelve percent return on my investment. Do you feel that you can deliver a twelve percent return on investment?"

She was kidding, right? She had to still be kidding. Any moment now she was going to laugh and throw another piece of cookie at his head.

"Yeah," said Justin. "Twelve percent. I mean, that's a fair request, I think."

There was no mirth in Grandma's eyes. "And you're willing to sign paperwork to that effect?"

"Yes, ma'am."

Gabe cleared his throat. "I think we should discuss this first."

Grandma nodded. "Very well. I'll go make more lemonade. You have five minutes."

Grandma stood up and walked out of the room. Gabe checked to make sure she was truly gone and then lowered his voice. "I don't want to owe your grandmother anything if the project falls apart."

"It's not going to fall apart."

"Movies fall apart all the time! We had a movie fall apart two days ago! A third of five thousand dollars is one thousand, six hundred, sixty-six dollars, and sixty-seven cents. I can't pay that back."

"Plus the twelve percent," said Bobby.

"Right. Plus the twelve percent."

"How much is that?"

"One thousand, eight hundred, sixty-six dollars, and sixty-seven cents."

"How'd you do that in your head?"

Gabe ignored him. "Justin, I want to help you make the movie, and I'm willing to do what it takes to raise the money. But I don't want to be in debt to anybody. I don't think it's even legal for us to promise her a return on her investment, and I don't think it's legal of her to demand one, so it's not like it would hold up in a court of law, especially since we're minors and this is a grandson-grandmother agreement. But still, my parents will *shred* me if I do something like this."

"I totally understand," said Justin.

"We can still do a bake sale," said Bobby.

"Oh, we will. But I'm going to accept the five thousand dollars, and I'll take the full responsibility for paying it back."

"What if the movie doesn't get finished?" asked Gabe.

"It will."

"Okay, but for the sake of argument, what if it doesn't?"

"That's not an option."

"It's not an option after your grandmother hires goons to break your legs, but right now we *do* have options, so let's discuss them."

"No safety net, remember? I'm making this movie. And it's going to be amazing. And if we can't earn back fifty-two hundred dollars, I deserve Grandma's wrath."

"Fifty-six hundred dollars."

"I thought you said your share would be one thousand, eight

hundred, sixty-six dollars, and sixty-seven cents? That's two hundred dollars more than… Oh, right, it's times three. Fifty-six hundred dollars is right. I'm still taking the money."

"Should I be knocking you unconscious and dragging you out of here for your own good?"

"Nah."

Gabe turned to Bobby. "Any thoughts?"

"I wish my grandmother would give me five grand."

"All right," said Gabe. "I've expressed my objections. You've officially ignored them, and we can move forward."

Grandma walked back into the living room with a fresh pitcher of lemonade. She refilled their glasses and then sat down on the piano bench. "So what did you boys decide?"

"We'd love to have you invest in our movie," said Justin. "I really appreciate this. I can't tell you how much it means to us."

"Oh, goody," said Grandma. "This is going to be so much fun." Again her eyes went ice-cold.

The eyes of a hardened killer.

The eyes of doom.

Suddenly Justin came up with the greatest movie idea ever. It would be a terrifying film about a grandmother who—

No, no. Focus. One project at a time.

6

JUSTIN, GABE, AND BOBBY SAT IN JUSTIN'S ROOM,

each typing away on their laptops.

Grandma's check was safely tucked away in Justin's wallet. For a split second, he'd thought that Grandma drew a skull underneath her signature, but it had just been his imagination.

Bobby snickered.

"Did you write a funny part?" asked Justin.

Bobby hesitated for a moment. "Yes."

"What was it?"

"It needs another draft or two before I'm ready to share it."

Justin stood up and walked over so he could see Bobby's computer. Bobby switched screens, but he wasn't fast enough to stop Justin from seeing that he wasn't working on the script. And the screen he switched to wasn't the script either. Bobby realized this and flipped to a third screen that also wasn't the script before he flipped back to the script.

"We're supposed to be working."

"I am working."

"You were watching a giraffe video."

"Research."

"Research for what?"

"A giraffe scene."

"C'mon, Bobby. We need to take this seriously."

"I *am* taking it seriously. Look how much I've written already."

"Two lines!" shouted Justin.

"Two *great* lines."

"We can't afford a giraffe," said Gabe.

"He wasn't writing a giraffe part. He was just watching a video."

"Not everyone can just turn on their inspiration like a light switch," said Bobby. "Some of us need to ease ourselves into creativity. Maybe you have your own little quirks. Do you hear me judging them? No. If I want to watch a giraffe steal a lady's jar of peanut butter to get in the mood to write, who are you to tell me it's wrong?"

"Does the giraffe really steal her peanut butter?" asked Gabe.

"Yeah. You want to watch?"

Three minutes and eighteen seconds later, Justin said, "Okay, yeah, that was a pretty funny video. But we're on a super-tight schedule, and we can't mess around."

"I think that video was faked," said Gabe. "Why would that lady be carrying around a whole jar of peanut butter at the zoo? Nobody does that."

"No more videos," said Justin. "No social media. Nothing but zombies, zombies, zombies until we're done."

"Can we watch zombie videos for inspiration?" asked Bobby.

"No," said Justin, but then he considered it. "Actually, maybe that's not a bad idea. We'll watch *part* of a movie just to get ourselves into the right mind-set."

"I vote the original *Dawn of the Dead*," said Gabe.

"I vote the remake," said Bobby.

Four hours later their double feature was over. Justin had only planned to watch the first ten minutes of each, but you couldn't just pop in the original *Dawn of the Dead* and not watch the whole thing. It was a good idea in theory but didn't actually work in the real world. And once they'd finished the original, they had to respect Bobby's wishes and watch just the first ten minutes of the remake, which then became just the first twenty minutes, which then became just the first thirty minutes, which would have become just the first forty minutes except that they completely lost track of time until the movie was over.

"Are we all inspired now?" asked Justin.

"I'm kind of hungry," said Bobby.

"Me too," said Gabe.

"Do you think your mom would make spaghetti?"

"I'll ask," said Justin.

They sat at the dinner table, eating spaghetti and meatballs. Justin noticed that one of his meatballs kind of looked like a brain, but he didn't share this observation with anybody because he didn't want to be asked to leave the table. Neither Mom nor Dad appreciated it when dinner was compared to internal organs.

"How's the script going?" Dad asked.

Bobby said, "Good." Gabe said, "Fine." And Justin said, "Eh."

"Five thousand dollars. Wow. Your grandmother never gave *me* five thousand dollars. I thought that she was going to give you forty bucks. Maybe fifty. Five thousand dollars. That's crazy."

Justin knew what was coming next. Three…two…one…

"What you should do is put that money toward your college education," said Mom.

"She wants it back after the movie comes out," Justin told her. "She's an investor, not a donor."

Dad, who'd been about to shove a large bite of spaghetti into his mouth, set his fork back down on his plate. He'd suddenly gone pale. "It wasn't a gift?"

"No. I told you that."

"Oh. I assumed it was a gift." He took a deep breath, closed his eyes, and exhaled slowly. He reopened his eyes and looked at Justin. "You *are* going to finish the movie, right?"

"Yep."

"Okay. Good." Dad shoved his plate away as if he'd lost his appetite. "Good."

After dinner they returned to Justin's room. They weren't anywhere close to finishing the script. Perhaps it had been too ambitious to think that they could write an entire feature film screenplay in one sleep-deprived day, especially a film that was supposed to redefine the genre for a whole new generation.

Still, he didn't have to wake up for school until 7:00 a.m. That left plenty of time if he didn't squander any of it by being unconscious. They could do this.

Clack clack clack clack, went Justin's keyboard.

Clack clack clack clack, went Gabe's keyboard.

Clack..................clack, went Bobby's keyboard.

"I think I need to get going," said Gabe, closing his laptop.

"All right," said Justin. He sighed. "We're off to a good start anyway. I mean, there's cool stuff happening in literally every paragraph."

"I kind of went with more character development."

"That's fine," said Justin. "Character development can be cool too. So we're still going to do this, right? All-nighters for everyone?"

"Yeah," said Gabe and Bobby, and they almost sounded like they kind of meant it.

His friends left, and Justin sat at his desk, staring at his computer screen. He'd wanted to write thirty pages today. He'd written eight. Well, seven and three-quarters, rounded up. Not bad for a regular day's work. But this was no regular day, and eight was not thirty. Twenty-two pages left to go. That seemed like a lot of pages.

It was six o'clock. That left thirteen hours until the alarm went off. Thirteen whole hours! So he didn't even have to write at the rate of two measly pages an hour to finish on schedule. Anybody could write two pages an hour. That was a full half hour per page. No problem at all. And if he wrote three pages an hour…or even four, he could get some sleep.

By seven o'clock he'd written another page and a quarter.

Not a big deal. He didn't have to write two pages every single hour to finish on time. He just needed to *average* two pages an hour. He could make up for the previous hour's shortfall by accelerating his pace throughout the upcoming hour, which would be really easy once he built up some momentum.

Then Mom made him take out the garbage and recyclables, which messed up his momentum.

Mom and Dad were watching a television show that looked highly entertaining, but Justin resisted the temptation to join them and returned to his room.

By eight o'clock he hadn't written much more. He wouldn't count that against himself because of the distraction with the garbage, which wasn't his fault. He'd get it done. He'd been in this position many times. He worked best under pressure.

Did they really need to get the movie shot before Gabe left for the summer?

Justin was appalled at himself for allowing that traitorous

thought to creep into his mind. Of course he did. They were a team. He didn't want to make the movie without him. They'd been best friends forever. And though Gabe's job was to be the voice of reason, Justin knew that he'd be genuinely heartbroken if they finished the movie while he was gone.

Making the movie without Gabe was not an option. The only options he needed to worry about right now were these: Coffee or Red Bull?

Maybe both.

The surgeon general would probably say, "Goodness, no, you shouldn't have coffee and Red Bull at the same time!" but the surgeon general didn't have a screenplay to write, so he could just keep his whiny opinions to himself.

He wrote for another two caffeine-free hours, racking up four unspeakably awesome new pages. After Mom and Dad went to bed, he went into the kitchen and made a cup of coffee with the Keurig. Then he grabbed a Red Bull out of the refrigerator and returned to his room.

He chugged the Red Bull in a few quick gulps, took a sip of coffee, and returned to work. He was sooooo tired, but artificial stimulants would take care of that problem. A couple of minutes later, he'd finished the cup of coffee too.

```
Veronica punches the zombie in the face, causing
its eyeballs to pop out and dangle from their
stalks. The eyeballs bounce against each oth-
er a couple of times before the zombie falls to
the ground.

A noise behind her! Veronica spins around and
```

```
gasps in horror as a zombie in a lion tam-
er's outfit reaches for her with both hands
andddddddddddddddddddd
```

Justin snapped awake. He needed another Red Bull.

If Mom or Dad weren't asleep, one or both of them would probably try to dissuade him from the decision to consume another energy drink. So he was glad that they were asleep. He needed wings.

He went to the kitchen, got another Red Bull out of the refrigerator, and gulped it down. Oh yeah. He could feel the creativity flowing through his veins already. Every blood cell, both white and red, was electrified with pure energy. With this much power at his disposal, maybe he'd crank out *two* movie scripts tonight!

Ha-ha. He was just joking with himself. He'd stick with the one script as planned.

His right pinkie was twitching. Good. It could tap the keys faster.

Ah, so that's what a rapid heartbeat felt like! He'd always kind of wondered. This project was giving him the opportunity to enjoy all sorts of new experiences.

```
...reaches for her with both hands and misses.
Veronica slams her forehead into the zombie's
forehead. Her forehead is much more durable, and
the zombie's head shatterslikeglass.
```

Space bar. He had to remember to use the space bar.

Despite all of this awesome energy, Justin still felt exhausted like he'd been running for several miles but couldn't stop because some guy with a machete was still chasing him. He couldn't figure out if his body was awake and his brain was tired or vice versa.

Now his left pinkie was twitching. That would help balance things out.

```
...shatters like glass. The zombie falls to the
ground. Veronica steps on what's left of its head
as she walks away.
```

VERONICA

```
        I'm so very tired. Oh, to
        sleep!

        How wonderful it would be to
        sleep!
```

Justin wondered how Gabe and Bobby were doing. Both of them should be awake, so texting them wouldn't disturb them. But they might be in the zone. It wasn't cool to interrupt somebody who was in the zone. When he got into the zone later tonight, he wouldn't want either of them breaking his concentration. The zone was crucial if they were going to finish this screenplay before school tomorrow.

Before school *today*, technically.

Those blankets on his bed sure looked enticing. They were the same blankets he'd had for the past three or four years, but they seemed different somehow. Warmer. Fluffier. Comfier.

Had his blanket just moved?

Justin swore the blanket had turned down a bit at the corner, inviting him underneath the covers.

No! He had to resist!

He'd been in this situation many times. "Oh, why didn't I start studying for that test a week ago?" he'd often wail. "I could've studied for a mere fifteen minutes a day and my life would be wonderful! But now…oh, the misery of my existence!" But he always got the studying done. And this was for something that he liked a lot more than math. He'd fight through this. He'd get his third of the script done, no matter what.

You don't need to write that script tonight, his bed said in a low purr. *We haven't been spending enough time together. Don't you love me anymore? Just slip between the sheets and close your eyes, and the script will be magically finished when you wake up.*

His bed was lying to him. Justin would not be fooled.

I would never lie to you, his bed assured him. *We're the best of friends forever. You know you're sleepy, and I'm as cozy as snuggling with a hundred kittens. Come on, Justin. I have your best interests at heart. Trust me.*

You can totally trust him, said the pillow. *Just one hour of sleep. That's all you need. Think how much more productive you'll be if you get in that one short hour. I'm the softest, most wonderful pillow in the world. Why would you want to break my fluffy little heart?*

Justin was not going to let them win this battle of wills. He was going to write all night, and no inanimate object—a bed for example—was going to break him.

"That's enough out of you," Justin said, but not out loud because otherwise he'd be speaking to a bed.

You've just made a powerful enemy, his bed said with a snarl. *You'll regret your disloyalty! The next time you get in me, I'm going to bite you in half! Right in half with my sharp, glistening fangs! Ha-ha-ha-ha-ha! By the way, there's a scary clown in your closet.*

At least his pinkies weren't twitching anymore.

No, wait. Maybe his eyeballs were twitching, and that just made his pinkies look normal.

Veronica sees another horde of zombies coming toward her. But unlike the other zombies she's killed today, these are running! Jeez, am I tired. How can I be so alert and yet so tired at the same time? I think I can actually feel my pancreas working. Does this stuff I'm typing right now count as official productivity? Probably not.

So tired.

So very tired.

So......................

7

WHEN JUSTIN'S ALARM WENT OFF, IT STARTLED him so badly that he almost fell out of his chair. He'd written thirty-three pages. His sense of accomplishment faded a bit as he scrolled through the script and discovered that most of them were the phrase *want to sleep cannot sleep want to sleep cannot sleep want to sleep bed will eat my head* typed over and over in various fonts. After he deleted the evidence of his madness, he was left with twelve pages.

No big deal. When he added that to whatever Gabe and Bobby had written, they'd have a pretty big chunk of the script completed. It would at least be enough to prove to Alicia that he was serious.

In the shower he could feel each individual droplet of water pound into him with the force of a stampeding rhinoceros. He couldn't believe how terrible he felt. It was almost as if the human body required sleep to function properly.

He looked in the mirror. Ugh. There was a reason he worked *behind* the camera.

"You look tired," Mom said as he sat at the dining room table and poured himself a bowl of Extreme Sugar Flakes.

Justin said, "Yeah," or something approximating that.

"Didn't sleep well?"

Justin shrugged. Or at least he thought he shrugged. His body made some sort of twitching movement at any rate.

He only lived four blocks from school, so every day he walked instead of taking the bus. Normally this was a good thing since buses were often filled with students who liked to flick Cheetos and/or boogers at you, but today he would have appreciated the ride. Or even better, he would love for someone to just carry him to school on a stretcher.

Gabe, who lived only two blocks farther from school, was waiting outside when Justin left the house. He looked absolutely exhausted but didn't look crazed, so he must have gotten some actual sleep.

"How'd it go?" Justin asked.

"At three in the morning, I had to crash," Gabe admitted. "I ended up with fifteen pages. Half of what I was supposed to write. I'm sorry."

"I only did twelve."

"Slacker."

"What do you think the odds are that Bobby wrote sixty-five pages?"

"Not great."

"What do you think the odds are that Bobby wrote thirty pages?"

"Not great."

"What do you think—"

"We both know he went home and went straight to bed," said Gabe.

"Yeah," said Justin. "He's so lucky."

Bobby, who took the bus and often had Cheetos stains on the

back of his shirt, was hanging out by the Squid Hand Tree, which was so named because Gabe thought it looked like a squid and Bobby thought it looked like a hand. (Justin thought it looked like a fork, but that observation had not been incorporated into the tree's name.)

"Hey, guys," Bobby said. "You look tired."

"Yeah," said Gabe, and Justin merely nodded because it required less effort.

"Did you get your shares done?"

"No," said Gabe. Justin shook his head.

"You didn't?"

"Did you?"

"Yeah." Bobby looked surprised. "That's what we were supposed to do, right?" He unzipped his backpack and took out a stack of pages. "I even printed out three copies for us to review during lunch. Why did I bother staying up all night if you guys weren't going to pull your own weight?"

"Let me see that," Justin said and took the pages from him. He quickly flipped through them. They were indeed the pages of a zombie screenplay. "How'd you do that?"

"I told you. I just needed inspiration."

"Well, you got to write the last third, which has all of the coolest stuff," said Justin.

"What Justin means," said Gabe, "is that we both apologize and that we're glad at least one of us did what he was supposed to do."

"Yeah," said Justin. "I'm sorry. I'm really tired, and last night I hallucinated that my bed threatened to eat me."

Bobby shrugged. "It's okay. Sometimes beds are jerks."

"I'll try to write a couple of pages during first period."

"During the test?" Gabe asked.

Justin stared at Gabe for a very long time. "Test?"

"The history test. Today. First period."

Justin suddenly wished there was a nearby bunker where he could hide away for a few minutes and scream. "I completely forgot to study for that! Why didn't you remind me?"

"I studied last week."

"Studying last week doesn't count! People only remember stuff if they look at it the night before!" Justin wanted to weep, but again there was no bunker.

"I guess I just assumed that you wouldn't spend all day yesterday working on the script if you didn't feel prepared for the test."

"Oh, really? You didn't think I'd make a poor decision? You know me better than that! We've been friends for a hundred and fifty years!" He let out an exasperated sigh. "I guess I'll try to work on the script during second period."

Mr. Dzeda handed the tests to the first person in each row for them to pass back. Justin's stomach felt like it was filled with writhing slugs.

"Remember," said Mr. Dzeda, "this is an open-book test."

Open-book test! Open-book test! Justin was saved!

Where was his book?

Justin didn't think he'd performed very well on the test, but he'd stayed conscious the whole time, which was its own victory.

In second period Ms. Spitler caught Justin passing a note to Bobby that contained a particularly awesome zombie demise. Her policy was that if you got caught passing a note, you had to read it in front of the class. That policy no longer applied to Justin because it had worked out poorly for Ms. Spitler in the past. Instead she just scowled at him.

He'd hoped for a rare Alicia sighting, but he didn't pass her in the hallway. She had the earlier lunch, so he didn't see her there either. He sat down with Gabe and Bobby to discuss the script in progress.

"Did you make your own lunch?" Bobby asked Justin.

"Yeah, why?"

"You packed a box of baking soda."

"Yes, well, as I said, it wasn't a restful night."

"Are you going to eat the baking soda?"

"No."

"I'll give you a buck if you do."

"No, thank you."

Bobby handed each of them a copy of the last third of the script. "Remember, this is a first draft. There may still be typos and continuity errors."

"No, this is great," said Justin, skimming it. "This is really great. This is…" He trailed off.

"What?"

"This is *Dawn of the Dead.*"

"No, it's not."

"It is. It's the *Dawn of the Dead* remake."

"It is not. *Dawn of the Dead* doesn't have a character named Veronica Chaos."

"I'm not saying that you did a cut-and-paste, but look at this." Justin held up one of the pages. "It's right out of *Dawn of the Dead*."

Bobby looked over the page and then frowned. "Hmm. I guess I was more inspired than I thought."

"I take back my apology," said Justin.

"Sorry, guys," said Bobby. "No wonder it went so smoothly."

"I wish you were smarter," said Justin.

Gabe took the pages from Bobby. "Knock it off. We all messed up. Instead of focusing on what we didn't get done, let's focus on what we did. We still have almost thirty pages of script, so that's half an hour of the movie, and we know enough about the characters to start the rest of the casting. I'll put up signs around the drama department to let them know that we're holding auditions tomorrow right after school."

"What we need to do is find people with really strong improv skills," said Justin. "We wanted actors who were going to elevate the material beyond the printed page anyway."

"So you're suggesting making the movie without a completed script?"

"No, I'm suggesting letting the cast write the rest of the script. On the set. While we're filming."

"But you said—"

"Stop quoting me back to me," said Justin. "I say stuff, and then I say stuff later that contradicts it. I'm aware of that personality trait, and I accept it."

"I just feel like maybe we're cutting corners."

"We're not cutting corners. We're embracing innovation. Remember how you wanted to have eighteen different actors play the vampire? I shot that down because it was a stupid idea. But it was a *creative* idea, and I know that if we'd kept brainstorming, you would have come up with an idea that wasn't stupid. Let's play to our strengths."

"We're cutting corners."

"We're being flexible."

"Flexible would be letting the actors change lines in a script that are already written."

"You're being inflexible by insisting that we're cutting corners."

"But we are, and you know it."

"Don't tell me what I know."

"Guys, calm down," said Bobby. "Cutting corners is part of the filmmaking process. There's a long, proud history of cutting corners to get a movie made. Everyone does it except Pixar. All in favor of letting the actors improvise, raise your hand."

Justin and Bobby raised their hands.

"So we're a democracy?" asked Gabe.

"Yes," said Justin.

"Even though you were the one who was always in charge? Because that means you're giving up power."

"Stop trying to hurt my brain," said Justin.

"All right," said Gabe with a shrug. "If I'm outvoted, I'm outvoted."

"No, wait," said Justin. "I changed my mind. I'm the director, so I should have the power. We'll finish the script tonight."

"Okay. And we need permission to film in school after hours."

"I've got it covered," said Justin.

Gabe looked over at Bobby. "Find out if your uncle Clyde can do special effects."

"You're not going to do them?" Bobby asked.

"I won't have time. And I can really only do basic stuff.

We need somebody like Uncle Clyde if we're going to have professional-looking zombies."

"Isn't he still in jail?" Justin asked.

"Nah," said Bobby. "He got out a couple of months ago."

"I'm not sure we should have an ex-con working on our movie."

"Relax," said Gabe. "It was a white-collar crime. We just need to keep him away from our parents' taxes."

That seemed reasonable to Justin.

They made a list of everybody's additional jobs for the evening, which took the rest of lunch period to compile. Once again Justin considered that perhaps he'd bitten off more than he could chew.

But would a zombie worry that it had bitten off more than it could chew? No. A zombie would take the biggest bite possible, even if it didn't fit in its mouth, even if the zombie would choke if it tried to swallow the bite.

That was not a very good line of logic. No more energy drinks for the remainder of the project.

8

JUSTIN SAT OUTSIDE THE PRINCIPAL'S OFFICE. HE felt nervous even though he wasn't in any trouble. A couple of other students made witty comments as they saw him sitting there, and he explained that he was seeking a filming permit. But the witty students didn't seem to believe him.

"You can go in now," said Mr. Clark, who was Ms. Weager's administrative assistant. He had a ponytail and a goatee. He always tried to strike up conversations about video games and act like he was your best buddy. This was a stark contrast to Ms. Weager herself, who did not act like she was your best buddy, an average buddy, a casual acquaintance, or even somebody who didn't resent your existence on this planet. Her expression and body language said, *We both know that I'm not allowed to break a ruler over your head, but if legislation ever gets through congress allowing me to do such a thing, I'd advise you to invest in a helmet because I will beat you within an inch of your darn life. And the only reason I'm saying "darn" is because I'm the principal and I'm supposed to be setting a good example, but you can bet your bottom that I'm thinking a different word.*

Justin walked into Ms. Weager's office, which seemed to have been designed with an optical illusion that the walls were closing in. Unless the walls really were closing in, perhaps to discourage loitering.

Ms. Weager was all sharp angles. If you patted her on the shoulder, you would probably cut your hand. Justin had never seen a single strand of her hair move. Not only could it remain perfectly still in hurricane-force winds, but Justin suspected that you could bounce a roaring chainsaw off it and cause no damage.

"Please have a seat," she said.

Justin sat down in front of her black iron desk. Well, it wasn't really a black iron desk, but the way she sat made it look like something made out of black iron adorned with spikes and skulls.

The chair was not comfortable.

"What can I do for you?"

"My friends and I are going to make a feature film," said Justin. "And I wanted to get permission to film in the school."

"Won't that be disruptive to the learning process?"

"I meant at night. Not during school hours."

"What sort of movie?"

Justin had expected this question, and he knew that offering the full truth wasn't the way to go. But neither was it a good idea to lie to one's principal. So he said, "It's a social commentary."

"What sort of social commentary?"

Zombie movies often had the subtext of everybody acting the same and refusing to think for themselves. Ms. Weager didn't seem to be opposed to that concept. "It's about rule breakers," said Justin. "It deals with people who violate societal norms."

"In what way?"

By eating human flesh was not the correct answer here. "By violating taboos."

"If you're making a movie about taboos on school property, I need to know specifics."

"It's about people being given a second chance."

"Name the taboo."

"Poor nutritional choices."

"Is this a zombie movie?"

Suddenly Justin wondered if he'd misjudged Ms. Weager. Maybe she was a huge zombie movie fan. Maybe she came home after a long day of yelling at kids, plopped down on the couch, and put in her special edition Blu-ray of *Evil Dead 2*. And maybe she was geeky enough to know that the zombies in that movie weren't technically zombies but rather people who were possessed by the spirits of the dead.

"Yes," he said.

"Will there be blood?"

"A drop or two here and there, when it's relevant to the social commentary."

"I'm sorry. You won't be making a zombie movie on school grounds."

"But the zombies are a metaphor. Shouldn't we be learning about metaphors?"

Ms. Weager removed her glasses, which looked like they could double as a tool for gutting fish. "I appreciate your creativity," she said, sounding insincere. "But this is not appropriate material, and your request is denied."

Justin wanted to protest, but at the same time he didn't want her to push a button and open a trapdoor beneath him.

"Are you sure?" Justin asked. "I could write up a list of themes and stuff."

"I'm sorry. Let me know when you make a movie that's not about zombies."

Justin thanked her for her time and left the principal's office. A couple of other kids were seated outside, awaiting their grim fate. One of them was Patrick, who probably had his own "Reserved for Patrick Sartin" seat in detention. Usually he ended up in detention for mouthing off to teachers and for light vandalism, but he'd been suspended once for stealing somebody's jacket out of their locker. (He didn't even want it.) And there were rumors—though they were never confirmed—that he liked to start the occasional fire.

Mr. Clark told a pretty blond girl that she could go in to see the principal. She wiped a tear from her eye, went into Ms. Weager's office, and shut the door behind her.

Justin sat down next to Patrick. They'd shared a couple of classes and knew each other's names, but they weren't friendly enough that it was typical for Justin to sit down next to him and start talking.

"How's it going?" Justin asked.

"The usual."

"Can I ask you a hypothetical question?"

Patrick raised an eyebrow. Either he wasn't comfortable with hypothetical questions, or he didn't know what "hypothetical" meant.

"Purely imaginary," Justin assured him. "One hundred percent. This is only to satisfy my curiosity."

"Ask it."

Justin lowered his voice to a whisper. "Let's say that somebody wanted to in this completely made-up scenario...be inside the school during certain hours."

"You want to break into the school after dark?"

"No. Definitely not. I just want to know if such a thing is possible. It's research."

"Yeah, it's possible. When are we doing it?"

"We're not."

"How about tonight at ten? Can you sneak out?"

"Seriously. I'm just gathering information."

"I've got new spray paint. Eight different colors. I've got this turquoise shade that would go perfectly with the door to the chemistry lab."

"I wasn't looking for spray paint activities."

"I've got this realistic-looking plastic finger that we could drop into Mr. Schmidt's aquarium. It'll make people think the fish bit off somebody's finger. It's a great prank because it causes no harm to the fish."

"What if Mr. Schmidt thinks they're too vicious to live?"

Patrick thought about that. "Well, he'd figure out that it was a fake finger pretty quick. It's not squishy or anything. I don't think there's any real chance that anybody would seek revenge on the fish."

"Thanks for your help," said Justin. "I don't have any plans to use what you just told me, but it's good to know. I appreciate it."

"No problem."

"I hope you don't get into too much trouble for whatever you did."

"I taped a tuna sandwich underneath my desk on Friday."

"Why?"

Patrick shrugged. "Attention, I guess."

"Good luck to you."

"Thanks."

Justin walked down the hallway. If he were a superhero, he'd be Frustrated Man. (This was why he worked in the horror genre instead of making up superheroes.) Most of their amazing production value was supposed to come from filming in the school. And it was essential to the plot. What were they going to do without it?

He would never, ever consider breaking into the school, but it was nice to know that the option was available, even if he would never, ever consider following through on it. Still, having options was good.

When he reached his locker, Alicia was waiting there for him.

"Hi," he said, playing it cool. Cool people said hi without following it up with ninety seconds of babbling.

"Hi," she said. "How's the script going?"

"Amazeballs," said Justin, even though cool people probably didn't say amazeballs.

"I can't wait to read it!"

"I think you'll like it. You get to kill a lot of zombies. I mean, a *lot*. Record-setting. You'll be a question on *Jeopardy!* someday."

She grinned. Justin had now set his own record for most consecutive words spoken to Alicia in person. If they spoke any longer, he'd have said so many words to her that he couldn't even keep an accurate count of them. And he hadn't passed out! Last week he never would have believed that he could carry on a conversation with Alicia and not at least get a little dizzy.

"May I make a request about my character?"

"Sure, anything."

"Can she have purple hair?"

"Oh yeah, absolutely. That's how I pictured her anyway."

"And what about a Mohawk?"

"A Mohawk?"

Alicia ran her fingers through her long blond hair. "I've always wanted a purple Mohawk, but my mom won't let me get one. If it's required for the part though, she'll have to let me do it."

"Well, I mean, I wouldn't *make* you get a Mohawk just for the movie—"

"Put it in the script so I can show her. And make sure there are some parts where the other characters talk about it. She needs to see that it's essential to the role. Can you do that for me?"

"Yeah, if that's what you really want. I'll make it a crucial plot element."

"While you're at it, could you put in that her nose and eyebrow are pierced?"

"I guess I could do that too."

"Thanks!"

"But you can do fake piercings."

"That's no good. Put in a scene where somebody tugs on them."

"Won't that hurt?"

"Not a scene where somebody tugs on them *hard*. Just enough so my mom can see that we can't fake it."

"I'm not sure your mom will buy that," said Justin. "I don't think a director would ask an actress to really pierce her nose. If he did, she'd have a hole in her nose, and her next role could be, you know, a nun or something."

"My mom doesn't know how movies work. I really want to get my nose and eyebrow pierced. Don't ruin this for me."

"I won't. I'll make sure the movie can't get done without the piercings."

"Thank you!"

"I'll have the script for you tomorrow."

"Can't wait!"

9

WHEN JUSTIN GOT HOME, HE KNEW THERE WAS
no way he could get through the evening without a nap. So he
went upstairs, took off his left shoe, decided that his right shoe
was fine where it was, and flopped down on his bed. Fourteen and
three-quarters of a second later, he was asleep.

A zombie with a tire iron lodged in its skull stood next to his
bed, staring at him. But Justin was dreaming, so that was okay.

"G'day," said the zombie, speaking in an Australian accent.
"I'm your subconscious mind. While you lie 'ere, sleepin' peace-
fully, I'm gonna finish writin' your script for ya, mate."

"Really?" asked Justin. "Gee whiz! That would be swell!"

The zombie pulled a typewriter out of its ear and began to
quickly tap on the keys. "Writing, writing, writing. Oh, that was
a good part. Writing, writing, writing."

"I love you, Mr. Zombie Personification of My Subconscious Mind!"

"Psych!" The typewriter disappeared into a cloud of pink
glitter. "Write your own script! Don't make your brain do all
the work!"

A dozen zombie arms burst through Justin's mattress. They

grabbed him by the hands, feet, head, and tailbone and dragged him down into the darkness.

Good thing this is a dream, thought Justin. It would be really unpleasant to be dragged down into a dark, zombie-filled pit if it weren't part of a dream.

There wasn't a lot of room, what with all of the zombies squeezed down there. The pit underneath his bed had been designed to hold maybe twenty zombies, twenty-two at the most, but there were at least thirty down here, so it was a tight fit. Justin couldn't remember ever having had less elbow room.

"Hey, guys, we need to make space," said Justin.

"There's space in our stomachs!" said one of the zombies.

Justin felt kind of silly. He should have known that suggesting that they needed to make space would quickly lead to one of the zombies mentioning that there was available space in their tummies. The next part was not going to be fun.

"Nom nom nom!" said the zombies.

Justin woke up.

Or *had* he?

Well, he wasn't in a zombie pit being devoured, so presumably he'd woken up. He sat up, feeling surprisingly refreshed considering that he'd only been asleep for a couple of minutes.

He sat at his desk, feeling strangely inspired, and began to type.

And he didn't stop until the first third of the script was complete.

(If you didn't count restroom breaks, dinner, a couple of mandatory household chores, homework, a few text message exchanges with Gabe and Bobby, a bit of TV watching downstairs so that his parents didn't feel abandoned, a cursory brushing of his teeth, and two more naps.)

Still, before his alarm clock made its horrific bleating sound to let him know that it was time to get ready for school, he was done!

He was so happy that he wanted to dance. So he did.

"What are you doing?" asked Mom, peering suspiciously into his bedroom.

"Dancing with joy."

"That doesn't look like any dancing I've ever seen. It's more like staggering."

"I haven't slept much."

When he met Gabe outside, Gabe said that he, too, had finished his third of the screenplay. "It was weird," said Gabe. "I had this dream where an Australian zombie said that he'd finish writing it for me."

Justin gaped at him. "Seriously?"

"No. You texted me about your dream in the middle of the night."

"Oh, that's right."

When they met him in front of the school, Bobby revealed that he had also finished his portion. "It wasn't easy," said Bobby. "There were times, especially 4:13 a.m., that I wanted to give up. But I didn't. I just took a deep breath, focused, and stuck my tongue in the connector of a nine-volt battery to give me the jolt I needed to keep going."

"I can't believe it," said Justin. "We've got ninety-seven pages here! We decided to make a feature film on Saturday night, and on Tuesday morning, we've got a completed screenplay! We're geniuses!"

"We're idiots," said Justin.

They sat in the lunchroom, reading through their script. The biggest problem with the script was that it was terrible. Unfortunately that was only one problem of many. It was also, in Gabe's words, "One hundred percent unfilmable on our budget."

"Not a hundred percent," Justin insisted.

"Fine. I was exaggerating. But it's close."

"If you're going to be an effective producer, you can't exaggerate. You have to stick to facts. If you gave inaccurate numbers on the set, a stunt could go wrong, and somebody could die."

"Then I won't give a percentage. It's completely unfilmable. There. Happy?"

"Why is it unfilmable?"

"Because it would cost trillions of dollars to make!"

"Didn't we just have a discussion about exaggerating?"

"I could open up this script and point to any random part, and there's going to be something that's too expensive for us to do." Gabe pulled a page out of the middle of the pile, closed his eyes, and then touched it with his index finger. He opened his eyes again. "Oh, look. I just touched a part where a burning Jeep drives off the top of a fast-food restaurant! How are we going to do that, Justin? Do you have a Jeep in your garage that we can set on fire? Do you know any fast-food restaurants that will be cool with us driving a Jeep off their roof? Should we just strap Bobby into the driver's seat and wish him luck? Hey, if he dies in a gruesome 'burning Jeep drives off a restaurant' accident, maybe it'll drum up some free publicity!"

"Now you're exaggerating *and* being sarcastic. What's your deal today?"

"My deal is that you didn't give any thought to what we could actually accomplish. You wrote this script like it's *Star Wars* with zombies."

"Oh, wow, that would be—"

"I knew that we were going to have to scale things back, but you didn't even try to be realistic. This isn't something we're going to play out in your backyard with action figures. It's supposed to be a real movie. Do you actually think that Alicia is going to let us give her a purple Mohawk?"

"She asked for that."

"Really?"

"Yeah."

"Oh. Okay. But nothing else is realistic."

"For the record, I never thought we were going to drive a real Jeep off a real restaurant and really set it on real fire. It's all CGI. CGI is free!"

"Bad CGI is free. Are we making a cartoon now? We can't do even one percent—and I'm not exaggerating this time—of the stuff that's in the script and make it look decent. Since when are we masters of special effects?"

"I'm reaching for the stars."

"Do you want to know the problem with that?" asked Gabe. "The stars are really, really, really, really, really, really high up. Do you know what the closest star is? The sun. Do you know how far away the sun is?"

"I can look it up," said Bobby, taking out his cell phone.

"It's almost ninety-three million miles away." Gabe pushed back his chair and stood up. He reached one arm up toward the ceiling and started jumping into the air. "Look at me! I'm trying to grab the sun! Oooh, just missed! Just missed again! Maybe this next jump will be ninety-three million miles high! Nope, not that one."

Justin glanced nervously around the lunchroom. Other kids were staring. It wasn't like Gabe to do things that attracted this kind of attention, so he must've been really upset. "You've made your point. Sit down."

Gabe sat down. "If you did touch the sun, it would melt your hand off, but that's irrelevant."

"I understand how the sun works."

"It's ninety-two million, nine hundred, and sixty miles away," said Bobby, looking at his cell phone.

Gabe ignored him. "We should be ambitious, but not to the point of self-delusion. If we try to make this script the way it's written, we'll be laughed out of town. And then we'll be laughed out of every other town with Internet access."

"Everyone is laughing at you already for trying to jump up to the sun."

"They're not laughing. They're staring. Do I regret jumping up in front of everybody and pretending that I was trying to grab the sun? Yes. But did I make my point? Yes."

"You certainly did."

"Also, the script bites."

Justin nodded. "Yeah, it does."

"My part too?" asked Bobby.

"All three parts," said Justin.

"But my part was the best, right?"

"No, your part was the worst."

"I don't agree with that," said Bobby. "I think Gabe's part was the worst."

"Why? Because mine had all the character development?"

"Yes. It would've been fine if it was in Justin's section at the beginning, but half an hour into the movie nobody wants to see that."

"Not true. The whole script is bad, but my middle section is the least bad."

"Your section is the second least bad," said Justin. "But we're still talking about tiny degrees of awfulness. I've got to say, guys, I'm disappointed in all of us."

"But me the least, right?" asked Bobby.

"No, you the most. We've already established that."

Bobby looked sad.

"I think what we've shown here is that trying to write a script in two days with no sleep doesn't give you the best end result," said Justin. "Still, I think we have a solid foundation."

"We don't have a solid foundation," said Gabe. "We have quicksand."

"Okay, you're done saying negative things for the rest of this meeting. The next time you have something negative to contribute, say, 'Happy dancing panda,' instead."

"All right."

"If we scale things back to accommodate our budget, tweak some of the dialogue, and get rid of a couple of the dumber plot twists, we'll be fine."

"Happy dancing panda," said Gabe.

"Yes, we all wrote some lines that human beings would be embarrassed to say out loud, some of us more lines than others, but the framework is there."

"Happy dancing panda."

"The script isn't perfect. Nobody is claiming that it is. But underneath the blobby layers of incompetence is the skeleton of something that could be amazing," said Justin.

"Happy dancing panda."

"Enough. The next time you need to say, 'happy dancing panda,' say, 'fluffy snuggly malamute.'"

"I'm done complaining for now," said Gabe. "Next topic—what did Ms. Weager say about us filming in the school?"

JUSTIN SHIFTED A BIT IN HIS CHAIR. "EXCUSE ME?"

"You were supposed to get permission to film in the building."

"Right."

"Did you?"

This felt like a situation where one lie could turn into another lie, and that could turn into another lie and another and another until he was buried beneath an avalanche of deceit. In most cases, being buried beneath avalanches of deceit was not the way to go. This was the time to be truthful and explain to his partners that Ms. Weager had denied his request.

Except that…

No. No "except that."

Except that…knowing they lost their primary location would be a major blow to their morale at a time when their morale was already suffering from the whole "our screenplay is awful" thing. What if they decided to pull the plug? Justin couldn't let that happen. He'd only spoken to Ms. Weager once. Maybe she'd just been in a foul mood. Maybe her water heater at home was broken, and her frustration had taken the form of disapproval of zombie cinema.

He'd talk to her again and do a better job of pleading his case.

In the meantime, why add stress to Gabe and Bobby's lives? They had enough stress already. It would be irresponsible to add more. Only a total *jerk* would add more. He had this completely covered, no problem at all, so there was no conceivable reason to instill gastrointestinal distress into his best friends over this particular issue.

"Yep," he said. "We're fine."

"We're fine" was not technically a lie because they were fine. He'd get permission. First thing tomorrow, when she was beginning instead of ending a day of dealing with unruly students, he'd talk to her. She'd change her mind. Definitely. There was nothing to worry about. Justin was sure of it.

"Yep," on the other hand, technically *was* a lie because it was in direct response to Gabe's question about whether he'd gotten permission to film in the building. However, if Gabe called him out on it, Justin could pretend to misremember the conversation and say that his answer of yep had been because he thought Gabe was asking if he'd talked to Ms. Weager, not if she'd actually given permission, which was still a lie but a little white lie.

If she said no a second time, he'd blurt out a tearful confession to Gabe and Bobby and deal with their reactions tomorrow. Until then, he was going to be optimistic. Everything would work out perfectly.

"Anyway," Justin said quickly but not so quickly that it would seem like he was trying to change the subject, "back to the script. We can still do the auditions today. I think we're all underestimating how much an actor can bring to the role if they're not locked into the words on the page. Why handcuff them? Why chain them to a big rock and throw it in the lake? We have genuinely talented people at our disposal, so what's the point of turning them into mindless robots? Let them bloom."

"Fine," said Gabe. "They can bloom."

"The script needs tinkering, but that's no reason to hold up the rest of the production. I think we're in good shape to move forward."

"I'll go along with that," said Gabe, "on the condition that we all make a solemn vow that nobody but the three of us will ever see this version of the script. I mean, nobody. It would be disastrous. It doesn't have to be a blood vow where we cut our palms and press them together, but it has to be a really serious vow. I mean it. I'm not playing around."

"I vow," said Bobby.

"I vow too," said Justin.

"Didn't you tell Alicia that you were going to give her the script today?" Bobby asked.

Justin frowned. "Yeah, I did. She's going to think I'm unreliable if I don't give it to her like I promised."

"Let her think that," said Gabe.

"I can't."

"Yes, you can. No good can come from letting her read it. Pretend it's got an ancient spell that summons evil spirits to our plane of existence. Don't be the guy who lets people read the ancient evil book, Justin."

"I have to give her the script. She has to know that I'm a guy of my word."

"Catastrophe," said Gabe. "Fiasco. Debacle. Cataclysm."

"Fluffy snuggly malamute," said Bobby.

"It'll be fine," Justin assured them. "I'll figure something out."

"Here you go," said Justin, handing Alicia the script.

"*Untitled Epic Zombie Movie*," she said, glancing at the title page. "Still trying to think of a name?"

"Yeah."

"How about calling it *Veronica Chaos*?"

"Maybe."

"*Veronica Chaos, Zombie Slayer*."

"Still maybe." Actually *Veronica Chaos, Zombie Slayer* sounded kind of cool, but he was already testing Gabe and Bobby's patience and didn't want to commit to a final title without running it by them.

"I'll read it as soon as I…" She flipped through a few pages. "Ummm, everything's blacked out with Magic Marker."

"Not everything."

Alicia read aloud. "*Veronica Chaos, fifteen and stunningly beautiful even with all of the lacerations covering her body, crawls out, wearing a shredded white wedding dress. She's holding a cat. She has a purple Mohawk, a pierced eyebrow, and a pierced nose.* That's all there is."

"Actually, the cat probably won't make the final draft. Cats aren't cooperative."

"Why did you cross it all out?"

"My partners and I are concerned about script leaks. Unfortunately these days it happens all the time. Scripts are getting leaked to the world before you've ever started the first day of shooting. It's a constant headache for people in our industry."

Alicia continued flipping through the pages. "Then, um, why did you give me the script?"

"I promised that I would. It's not you that I don't trust," Justin assured her. "It's just that we can't let our guard down. I'd do the same thing for Jennifer Lawrence."

"I'm not offended," said Alicia. "I'm confused."

"I wanted to prove that the script was done. And you'd said that you needed your mom to see the part about the hair and body modification."

"You could have just given me that page. This isn't very environmentally friendly."

"You're right. It's not," Justin admitted. "But it's the way Hollywood does it."

"Are you sure you're not thinking of the FBI?" She smiled when she said it. Her tone of voice implied, *I'm amused by you, and perhaps even a little charmed, but don't push it.*

"Hollywood and the FBI work in similar ways," said Justin, whose brain was screaming for him not to push it, while his mouth fearlessly forged onward. "It all seems kind of ridiculous, but if we get hacked, it can sink the whole project."

"How would they hack a paper printout?"

Justin didn't recall having been such a terrible liar in the past. Maybe he always had been but only lied to people who didn't challenge his truth.

His mouth started to offer some sort of explanation involving satellite photography, but his brain successfully deflected it in time. "You're right," he said. "That was kind of silly. I wasted a lot of paper and went through two Magic Markers. It wasn't a good use of our planet's limited resources. Maybe you should…"

Justin was going to suggest that Alicia become one of their producers. His brain, which was on high alert, tackled the thought and held it down until it lost consciousness.

"…be the production's environmental awareness consultant?"

"Nah," said Alicia. "I care about the environment a lot, but I also litter."

"Really? I litter too!"

"Seriously?"

Justin's shoulders slumped, and he shook his head. "No, I don't. I'm sorry."

"It's okay."

"Anyway, I hope you enjoy the script."

This was exciting. They'd never done an actual casting session before.

Justin's traditional casting process was to go up to one of his friends and say, "Hey, wanna be in my movie?" But for this project, he needed more actors than he had friends. And unlike previous ventures, this film would require actors with talent.

He, Gabe, and Bobby sat behind a small desk in a conference room in the library. About thirty kids were outside the room, studying the page of hastily rewritten dialogue they'd been given. As far as Justin could tell, they were all from the drama club. He'd hoped for more of a variety, perhaps a few football players or even a standard-issue bully, but he could definitely work with what he had.

11

"NAME?" JUSTIN ASKED.

"Tina Smith."

"Do you like zombie movies?"

"If they're not too bloody."

"This one may be bloody. Is that an issue?"

"Nah."

"You personally may be covered in blood," said Justin. "Are you okay with that?"

"How much?"

"It could be a few bathtubs full."

Tina smiled. "That's fine."

"Name?"

"Butch Jones."

"Do you like zombie movies?"

"Do *you* like zombie movies?"

"Yes," said Justin. "Very much."

"Then yeah, they're okay, I guess. How big is my part?"

"Name?"

"You know my name."

"For the record."

"We've known each other since fourth grade."

"This is for everybody's benefit."

"I've known Gabe and Bobby just as long."

"Right, but we're following an official process here, so I'll need you to state your name."

"I feel that if you're asking me for information that everybody in the room already knows, you're not making the most efficient use of our time. Time is a precious resource on a movie set."

"Are you just trying to make your audition memorable?" Justin asked.

"I could be."

"It's not going to work. State your name."

"I'm not going to do that. You know my name. Gabe knows my name. Bobby knows my name, and I know my name. Why pretend otherwise?"

"Because that's what actors do. They pretend."

"I prefer to pretend things that are realistic."

"This is a zombie movie."

"Even zombie movies need verisimilitude."

"I know what verisimilitude means," Justin informed him. "You said it hoping that I wouldn't know what it means, but I do."

"What does it mean?"

"It means that something appears true."

"Yep, you're right. Good job."

"And verisimilitude is more about believability than actual

truth, meaning that your acting is more important than the realism of the situation. So state your stupid name."

"Bob Jareth."

"That's not your name."

"But was it believable?"

"Next!"

"No, no, wait. I'll state my name. You were right. I was just trying to be memorable."

"Next!"

"Gary Weaton."

"Next!"

"C'mon, dude! I'm lovably quirky!"

"Next!"

"Name?"

"Brianna Booth."

"Do you like zombie movies?"

"Love 'em."

"Would you be willing to let us make a cast of your head?"

"How does that work?"

"We stick a couple of straws up your nose so you don't suffocate. Then we pour plaster all over your head, and you can't move for a couple of hours. Then we pry the mold off your face and use it to make a fake head that we can blow up."

"Does my shirt stay on?"

"Yes."

"I'm in."

"All right, Duane, read the lines off that sheet."

"Look out behind you! There's a—"

"This isn't a musical."

"I know that."

"You were singing the line."

"Oh, I didn't realize that."

"It's okay. Try again."

"Look out behind you! There's a—"

"Still singing."

"Could the character sing maybe?"

"No."

"Look out behind you! There's a zombie!"

"That's better, but you're still kind of doing it in a singsongy tone. What we're specifically looking for in our male lead is dialogue that's not in a singsongy tone."

Duane cleared his throat and nodded. "I can fix that. Just give me a second."

"Take your time."

"La la la la la la."

"The la la la's probably aren't going to help."

"I'm sorry. I'm used to auditioning for musicals."

"It's okay."

"Look out behind—"

"Still singsongy."

"Look out—"

"Still singsongy."

"Look—"

"Singsongy."

"What if I just play a zombie instead?"

"That's fine."

"Maybe we could have singing zombies," suggested Bobby.

"Don't talk during the auditions," Justin told him.

"All right, Amy, just read the lines off that sheet."

"Die, zombie! Die! Die! Die! Die!"

"Nice reading. However, the actual line is 'They've got us surrounded.'"

"I know that, but I don't want to play the character as a weak, helpless female."

"She's not weak. She's saying the line while she's smashing a shovel into the zombie's face."

"I feel like she would be overcome with animalistic fury. I just can't imagine killing a zombie without shouting, 'Die! Die! Die! Die.' I mean, in the real world."

"You know what? If you want to add, 'Die! Die! Die! Die!' to the line, that's totally fine, but also read the part that's on the paper."

"Do you have a shovel I could use to help get in character?"

"No."

"Anything I can swing?"

"We'd rather you didn't swing anything."

"Okay, I'll just mime it." Amy mimed swinging a shovel into a zombie's face. "Die! Die! Die! Die! Die! Die! Die! Die! Die! D—"

"I think we're fine with four dies."

"I wanted to give you more options in the editing room."

"I appreciate that, but we're not actually shooting the movie right now."

Amy glared at Justin. "I know that. I'm trying to demonstrate that during the making of your movie, I will give you more options in the editing room. I'm not some brainless bimbo who will just read the lines as they're written."

"Glare at us again," said Justin.

Amy glared at the three of them one at a time, left to right.

"Did you feel a chill?" Justin asked Gabe and Bobby.

"Yeah," said Bobby.

"You're genuinely scary," Justin told her. "You're cast."

"You should do a joke where the zombies are trying to eat this politician's brains and he's, like, so dumb that there's nothing to eat."

"Thank you. Next!"

"Name?"

"Chuck."

"Do you like zombie movies?"

"*The Walking Dead* is my favorite show. I know it's not a movie but whatever."

"That's fine."

"I saw Norman Reedus once."

"Seriously?"

"Yeah. He was grabbing a few napkins from the napkin dispenser. I remember thinking, 'Wow, that's Daryl Dixon from *The Walking Dead*, and he has to get his own napkins.' I would've thought he'd have someone to get them for him."

"I guess he's down to earth."

"I guess so. And it wasn't like he spilled something. It was just in case he needed to wipe his mouth. If I ever reach that level of fame, I'm totally making somebody wipe my mouth for me."

If you excluded the fact that the drama students were rather odd as a whole, it had been a pretty good set of auditions. Unfortunately they still didn't have anybody who could play the male lead. They needed an actor who was strong, handsome, and charismatic, someone had chemistry with Alicia.

He might be wrong, but Justin thought that he and Alicia had a decent amount of chemistry together.

Hmm.

"No," said Gabe.

"What?"

"You're not playing the lead."

"I never suggested that."

"You were going to."

"I didn't even open my mouth."

"You didn't need to. I saw the entire thought process go across your face, and I put a stop to it before it made it to your mouth."

"It's not an idea I ever would have proposed. You stopped it for nothing."

"That's fine. As long as we're all in agreement."

"I have enough challenges as the director. I can't add a leading acting role to my list of jobs. That would be crazy. If we had more prep time, maybe, but under these circumstances, no, I think it's best if I stay behind the camera."

"Also, you can't act," said Bobby.

"No, I *choose* not to act because of that traumatic moment in second grade when I wet my pants on stage in front of the entire school while I was playing the front half of a camel, which is what this whole conversation has been building toward, so I might as well put it right out there."

"I'd forgotten about the camel thing," said Bobby. "I'm not going to make any jokes. It was a very unhappy day for you."

"Less happy for the back half of the camel," said Gabe.

"That counts as a joke," said Justin.

Gabe shrugged. "Bobby took the pledge, not me."

"I'm not starring in the movie, okay? I was never going to suggest it. You guys are getting on my case for something I never said I wanted to do. I also never said that the actors should burp all of their lines. Want to get on my case for that?"

"I think we're all a bit stressed out," said Gabe. "Let's take five minutes to sit here silently and relax."

"We don't have time for that," said Justin. "We'll take two and a half."

Two and a half minutes and seven failed attempts to not talk later, they all took a deep, cleansing breath.

"You guys are going to think I'm kidding," said Bobby, "but the whole burping idea would actually be kind of revolutionary."

"I think we need the full five minutes," said Gabe.

Another two and a half minutes later, they all took another deep, cleansing breath.

"From this point forward, no more arguments," said Justin. "We all share one mind. If zombies eat one of our brains, they eat them all. We have to work toward a single, unified vision. Everybody in agreement?"

If either Bobby or Gabe had chosen this moment to make a hilarious comment about not agreeing with their need to agree, Justin felt like he might have genuinely lost his mind and started gnawing off his arm hair. Fortunately they both agreed, and his arm hair remained intact.

"So we still need our male lead. How do we find one?"

There was a knock on the door.

For a split second, Justin thought it was a zombie. This was ridiculous because (a) zombies did not exist, and if they did, (b) zombies would neither be inclined to nor possess the motor skills necessary to knock on a door. He was still very tired.

Justin got up and opened the door. It was Christopher Harrison.

Justin was not the type to writhe in jealousy over his class-mates. But if he *was*, he'd writhe in jealousy over Christopher Harrison. He was inarguably the most handsome kid in school. You could try to argue it, but you'd lose. Yes, concepts such as physical attractiveness are subjective by nature, but not in the case of Christopher. If you pointed to another student and said, "So-and-so is more handsome than Christopher!" everybody would look at you like you were stupid. You *weren't* stupid, not at all. You just obviously hadn't seen Christopher Harrison yet.

He wasn't the tallest kid in school, but if you wanted to elimi-nate the competition, it would only take a couple of head-flattening whacks with an oversized mallet to get him into the top spot. Every single tooth was glistening white, perfectly straight, and in the exact quadrant of his mouth where it belonged. His eyes—oh, his eyes—had such a glorious shade of blue. It was like he had twin miniature earths wedged into his eye sockets (but just the blue ocean part of the earth, not the brown land).

His hair was always perfect too. It looked as if he'd cut it three times a day. Top physicists would be baffled by its ability to remain perfect in all weather conditions despite the fact that it wasn't Lego-style helmet hair like Ms. Weager possessed.

His arms were muscular, perfect for removing zombie limbs.

He was an excellent speller. He'd never won a spelling bee, but when he lost, it was on words like *ukulele*, which was impossible to spell anyway.

And he was a nice guy. His aura of charisma was so intense that he could probably be a complete jerk and you'd still want to be by his side as he fled from a herd of rampaging bulls.

Though he was bad at geography, he was bad at it in an endearing way, and that one flaw made all of his other strengths shine that much brighter.

Nobody actually called him Christopher "Mr. Amazing" Harrison, but if somebody did, everybody else would nod and say, "Yep, that sounds about right."

"Hi," Christopher said, charmingly. "Are you still doing the movie auditions?"

"Yes," said Justin, Gabe, and Bobby.

"Well, then I'm here to audition."

"Great," said Justin. "Have you done any acting before?"

"Just when I forgot a homework assignment."

Everybody laughed.

"Seriously though. I haven't done much acting, but it's a skill I'd like to develop. If you cast me, I promise that I'll be completely devoted to your project. I won't let you down. When I commit myself to something, I'm like a Rottweiler with a marshmallow."

Justin handed him the script page. "Here are your lines."

Christopher glanced at the lines. Then he nodded and lowered the paper, apparently having already memorized them. "Behind you! There's a zombie!"

Bobby quickly glanced behind him and then looked embarrassed.

"Duck down and leave it to me," said Christopher. He pretended to raise a shotgun with such skill that Justin could practically see the shotgun in his hands. He mimed pulling the trigger, and Justin almost felt the chunks of the zombie's skull raining down upon the back of his neck.

"Sorry if any sludge got on you," said Christopher, and for an instant Justin thought he was talking to him instead of Veronica Chaos. "My name is Runson Mudd, and I've embraced this dark new world that we live in. Yeah, I miss the luxuries of running water and catering. But in this world, only the strong survive, and I am one of the strong. And I can see that you are one of the strong, so let's be strong together!"

A chill ran down Justin's spine. Gabe brushed a fingertip against the corner of his eye as if he was wiping away a tear.

"Thank you," said Justin. "Is it all right if my associates and I have a quick discussion?"

"Sure." Christopher left the room, shutting the door behind him.

"We're making a huge mistake," said Bobby. "He could change his mind while we're wasting time sitting here talking!"

"Everybody's cool with casting him, right?" asked Justin.

"Yeah," said Gabe. "He makes me want to be a better person. And that's perfect for the character."

Justin got up and opened the door again. "We'd love to offer you the role of Runson Mudd," he said as Christopher walked back into the room.

"Hey, great! What does it pay?"

"Screen credit and free sandwiches," said Justin.

"Bottled water?"

"Tap water in a bottle."

"My own trailer?"

"A place on the sidewalk where nobody else is standing."

"A personal assistant?"

"The world is your personal assistant."

"Cabbage?"

"You want cabbage?"

"No, not really."

"Okay."

"Do I get to be on the poster?"

Gabe fielded that question. "That's a creative decision that will be made by our marketing department, but yes."

"Who's playing Veronica Chaos?"

"Alicia Howtz," said Justin.

Christopher's already bright eyes lit up. "Really? She's playing my girlfriend?"

Justin coughed. "Well, we're still doing the final polish on the script. We're going to test out multiple variations of their relationship and see which one best suits our theme."

"That would be awesome if she played my girlfriend. I can totally see us being together. It just feels right."

"Yes," said Justin, "it would be delightful. I hope you like purple Mohawks. Anyway, we'll get back to you on that detail, but for now we're thrilled to have you on board."

12

"SOOOOOO," JUSTIN SAID AS HE, GABE, AND Bobby sat in his bedroom and worked on their laptops. "What if we tweaked the Veronica-Runson relationship so that they were brother and sister?"

"This is supposed to be the first time they met," said Gabe.

"Then long-lost brother and sister."

"Most of my character development is about their love story."

"We can work around that."

"No."

"We'd get rid of everything icky."

"Justin, do we need to have a discussion about priorities?"

"Nah."

"I feel like we do."

"No, no, no, you're right. You're right. You're right. It's *good* how easily I can picture them together. It's what we want. It's super way cool."

"I don't think they'll have that much chemistry," said Bobby.

"Of course they will! They'll have *scorching* chemistry! Every review will talk about it! I'm surprised they aren't already married!" Gabe declared.

"Maybe he'll have bad breath," said Justin.

"His breath is like roses. You smelled it," Bobby reminded him.

"It *was* pretty nice," Gabe admitted. "I wonder if he was chewing gum. Anyway, it's not like they're slobbering all over each other through the whole movie. There's one kiss at the very end, and they're both covered in guts, so Alicia probably won't be that into it."

"Yeah, I know. I have to focus on what's right for the movie. But can we get rid of the part where they cut off that zombie's head together using the same sword?"

"Would that change be right for the movie?"

Justin lowered his head. "No."

"Don't worry about it. Even the ugliest of directors have girl-friends. If we truly do make the greatest zombie movie ever, all three of us will have lines of women outside of our homes stretching for miles. We'll go broke buying new shirts to replace the ones that get ripped off our bodies by our adoring fans."

Justin grinned. "Then we should just go shirtless."

"No, we'd get all scratched up."

"The love story stays," said Justin. "I'm sorry about that. I won't have any more fits of jealousy."

They went back to working on the screenplay.

And by the time Gabe and Bobby had to leave, the three of them agreed that the script sucked quite a bit less.

"My nephew says you're looking for somebody to kill zombies for ya," said Uncle Clyde, who made everybody call him Uncle

Clyde, nephew or not. He inhaled from his e-cigarette and blew some vapor into the air.

"Movie zombies, yes," said Justin.

"You didn't need to clarify that, son," said Uncle Clyde. He took a sip from his latte and grimaced. "Ugh. I can't believe this is what passes for coffee these days. Disgusting. Why would anybody drink this?"

"You wanted to meet at a coffee shop."

"Yeah, because if somebody is going to buy me coffee, it might as well be expensive. Doesn't mean I like the taste." He took another sip, swished it around in his mouth, and swallowed.

"Anyway," said Justin, "Bobby and I are making a movie."

Uncle Clyde stroked his gray beard, which was practically long enough to conceal a sasquatch. "The noblest of professions."

"And like Bobby said, we need somebody to do the special effects."

One of the baristas walked over to their table. "Excuse me, sir. You can't smoke in here."

"I'm not smoking. I'm vaping."

"We don't allow either."

"There's steam coming out of my coffee!"

"I understand, sir, but you'll have to put it away."

"Fine, fine." Uncle Clyde tucked the e-cigarette back into his pocket and then looked over at Justin. "Do you smoke?"

"No, sir."

"Good. Nasty habit. Turns your lungs into sacks of black tar. I've smoked since I was twelve, and every morning I wake up hacking and coughing up blobs of this thick, oozy stuff that I'm sure is mucus but doesn't look like any mucus you'd find in nature."

"What does it look like?" Justin asked.

"You don't want to know, son. You don't want to know."

"Then why do you smoke?"

Uncle Clyde pointed to his face. "Do I look smart to you?"

Justin was unsure how to answer that and opted for the safety of silence.

"These days I vape. Comes in different flavors, every one of them vile. I'd get better flavor from chewing the armpits of a ninety-year-old baboon. And the nicotine addiction turns me into the kind of person who would snap at a coffee shop employee who's just doing her job. Don't smoke, Justin."

"I won't."

"Back to the topic at hand. Lucky for you, I'm between jobs at the moment."

"How far between?" Gabe inquired.

"Don't sass your elders, kid."

"That wasn't meant to be a sass."

"I am ready, willing, and available to work on your little movie, and I'll make the best zombies you've ever seen. I'll make zombies that'll make the ones on *The Walking Dead* look like a child's doll."

A lot of children's dolls were terrifying, but Justin didn't point this out. He knew what Uncle Clyde meant.

"I've run the budget, and for materials and labor, I can give you the super-special friend-of-my-nephew discount price of forty-nine hundred dollars."

Justin stared at him for a moment.

"Did Bobby tell you how much my grandmother gave me?"

"He might have. I don't recall."

"That's almost our entire budget."

"Okay, then if there's some left over, I'll throw in a fantastic Zombie Nose vs Apple Peeler effect."

"No, I mean, we need to save some of our money for other stuff."

Uncle Clyde took a sip of his coffee. "Ugh. This coffee is like dunking my tongue in a sewer rat's bathwater. Listen, son. You're trying to join the big leagues. Do you know what five grand will get you on a major production?"

"No, sir."

He held up his pinkie finger. "One finger. One *small* finger, not your index finger or anything like that. On a union movie, I paint this finger gray, and that's your five-thousand-dollar zombie effect. What you have to decide is if you're trying to make a real movie or you're goofing around with your buddies. Goofing around with your buddies is fine. I have fond memories of my buddies and me flinging firecrackers at seagulls. But call it what it is and don't act like you're trying to do something important."

Justin wasn't sure what to do. On one hand, Uncle Clyde was right. On the other hand, Uncle Clyde was a creepy, untrustworthy ex-con who would probably take the money and flee to another state.

"I won't be able to commit to allocating that much of our budget to special effects until I discuss it with my partners," said Justin. "I'll send you a copy of our final script in a couple of days with the effects portions highlighted. You tell me what materials you'll need, and we'll do some pricing."

"A real director wouldn't need to rely on his crew to make decisions."

"Technically the money part would be the producer's job."

"Don't act like I don't know the duties of the key filmmaking personnel. Do you know what a gaffer does? Do you?"

"He does the lighting."

"Well, hello, Mr. Wikipedia. I guess you're just a great big fountain of knowledge. I've got three other productions waiting on me for an answer, so if you're just here to waste my time, I'm going to have to consider my other options."

"Okay," Justin said.

"You're acting like you don't believe me."

"No, I believe you."

Uncle Clyde stroked his beard, shaking out some loose crumbs and an olive. He took another sip of coffee. "Ugh. This tastes like unwashed dirt. All right, I'll keep myself available for your cute little movie. I wouldn't do this for just anyone, but I like my nephew. Compared to my other nephew, he's pretty great. My other nephew, though…jeez. Bread changes color to help you know when it's not okay to eat, but does he understand that? Nope. Kid eats moldy bread. Does the taste clue him in that he's not doing the right thing? Nope. I once sat there and watched him eat seven slices of moldy bread. And he's an honor student. I think he needs more attention from his parents. He's sure not gonna get it from me."

"Uh, thanks?" said Justin.

"I once saw Kevin eat a bunch of moldy bread too," said Bobby. "It was pretty cool."

"Your uncle is weird," said Justin.

"Yeah," Bobby said with great pride.

"I won't lie and say that I don't have reservations about blowing almost our entire budget on zombie effects," said Gabe. "But the zombies are what it's all about, right? If we can talk him down to forty-five hundred so that we've got money left to rent prop weapons, then we should reluctantly do it."

"He won't let us down," said Bobby.

As they reviewed their latest rewrite of the script, Justin, Gabe, and Bobby were all thrilled to discover that it sucked even less.

They were not yet at the point where they were comfortable sharing their work with other human beings, but it was close enough that they could start putting together a tentative shooting schedule.

Midway through trying to figure out the schedule, which was about ten thousand times more complicated than they'd anticipated, they all despised one another, but they were friends again by the time they were done.

"My mom is letting me cut and dye my hair," Alicia said over the phone. "So thank you. This really means a lot to me. Your movie is going to change my life."

"You're welcome," Justin told her.

"I'm going to do it Friday night so it's fresh."

"Sounds great."

"Okay, talk to you later."

"Good-bye," Justin said since he couldn't think of a way to artificially lengthen the conversation. That was a skill he'd try to improve in the future.

Justin had to work on Thursday, so he scowled his way through an evening of manual labor while Mr. Pamm yelled at him. They needed to write a part in the script for Noisy Guy #1. As he worked, he revised scenes in his mind, trying to make the dialogue sparkle. He tried to occasionally sneak away so that he could write down some of his most clever ideas, but that was almost impossible with Mr. Pamm's extrasensory perception for slackers. Many of his thoughts were lost forever. RIP.

When he got home, Justin's body ached, but fortunately he didn't ache too much to move a mouse around and click some buttons, so he reviewed the newest drafts that Gabe and Bobby had emailed to him.

They sucked even less than before and almost sucked enough less that they didn't suck at all.

"We're actually going to do this," he said out loud.

"What was that?" Mom asked.

"Nothing. Just being creepy and talking to myself."

"All right."

Justin's palms were sweating. The screenplay wasn't perfect. It wasn't even close to perfect. Parts of it were still kind of terrible, especially the part Bobby wrote about a zombie goldfish. But with some on-the-set ingenuity and contributions by their talented cast, Justin was positive that they could turn this film into something truly spectacular.

He gave copies of the script to Alicia and Christopher, informing them that some parts were awful on purpose so that if the screenplay was leaked, they could identify which version of the script had been leaked and thus trace it to the leaker.

They were going to start production very early Saturday morning. Mr. Pamm had given him the day off…angrily. Justin would rather start on Friday night, but they'd be working sixteen-hour days Saturday and Sunday, and he didn't want to wear out his cast and crew. They probably didn't have the same level of endurance that he did.

These were going to be long days. Undoubtedly something would occasionally go wrong. He was prepared for that. His cast had no film experience, so he knew that one of the actors would mess up a line every once in a while, and he couldn't count on every single special effect working exactly as planned the first time. As good as Bobby was at holding up the boom mic, its shadow would get into the shot at some point, and Justin wouldn't lose his temper. He'd simply inform everybody that they would be doing a second take.

He hadn't quite figured out what to do about the school, but they wouldn't be using that location the first weekend, so he still had time to work it out. He was confident that the problem would be resolved in a completely satisfactory and legal manner.

Justin was ready to face any challenge. Solve any problem.

Justin Hollow was ready for anything.

"What history test?"

"I texted you a reminder last night," said Gabe.

"Didn't we just have one?" Justin asked. "How much history is there for Mr. Dzeda to test us on?"

"Did you study at all?"

"I can't do everything. Oh well, I guess I don't get to be a famous historian now."

"Don't be sarcastic. If we called Steven Spielberg, he'd tell you that you should've studied for the test."

He was right. Spielberg would be polite but firm. Justin needed to maintain his focus on academics, or the only movie he'd be making would be a documentary about living in a cardboard box in an alley, scavenging half-eaten lizards for his dinner, and burning his hair to stay warm.

"You've got to take this seriously," Gabe insisted.

"I am. I'm joking on the outside, but on the inside I'm throwing up."

"Um, throwing up, by definition, happens on the outside."

"When the movie is done, I promise that I'll think about that comment, and we'll both have a big laugh about how amusing it was. For now it's maybe not the best time to be correcting my puke comment."

"I wasn't trying to be amusing, but I get your point. If we hurry, you can cram in a few minutes of studying before he hands out the tests."

In the long, proud tradition of pretending that certain events in history never took place, Justin decided to pretend that the history test never happened.

13

"I HAVE A TITLE," BOBBY SAID AT LUNCH.
"Dead Skull."

"That's perfect," Justin said. "The instant we make a movie about a dead skull, that's the title we're going to use."

"I knew you were going to make fun of me," said Bobby. "That's why I made this poster to explain the concept."

He held up a sheet of paper. It was a drawing of the outside of the school with the title *Dead School* on the wall. The word *School* was then crossed out with spray paint and replaced with *Skull*.

"Dead Skull," said Bobby.

Gabe thought about it for a moment. "My mind says, 'No, that's dumb,' but my heart says yes."

"My heart says yes too," said Justin. *"Dead Skull* it is."

"For now," said Gabe.

"Right. For now."

"Because I'd like to believe that we'll come up with something better while acknowledging that so far we haven't."

"And if you say it really fast, it kind of sounds like *Dead's Cool,"* said Bobby.

"Dead Skull, Dead Skull, Dead Skull…no, it sounds like

Dead's Cull, which I guess could be like the culling of the grim reaper or something. *Dead's Cool* isn't a bad title actually, though I don't like it as much as *Dead Skull.*"

"What about *Dead Is Cool* without the contraction?" asked Gabe.

"I'm not sure our movie has any evidence that being dead is cool," said Justin. "Killing zombies is cool, yeah, but being dead is kind of a miserable existence. You're all rotted and stuff, and people are always trying to shoot you in the head."

"Fair enough."

"Thanks, Bobby!"

The night before he was to shoot his first feature film, Justin stood in his kitchen, making peanut butter sandwiches.

He was not a great chef by any stretch of the imagination. (He could make mushy macaroni and cheese or crunchy macaroni and cheese but nothing in between.) But a peanut butter sandwich did not exceed his skill level. The challenge was maximizing the number of sandwiches he could get out of his available peanut butter without being stingy to the point where somebody said, "Hey, there's insufficient peanut butter on this sandwich!"

He had dozens of small bags of assorted chips and a cooler full of bottled water, which were technically just bottles he'd refilled from the faucet.

And Mom had made cookies. Lots and lots and lots and lots of cookies. Cookies of almost every variety imaginable, except for peanut butter for obvious reasons. They had so many that by the end of the shoot, every member of the cast and crew would instantly become physically ill from the mere sight of a cookie. But it was a small price to pay for their art, and until that moment was reached, nobody would go hungry.

Though he had approximately 2,164,798 things to do before production began tomorrow, Justin was determined to get a good night's sleep. He could sleepwalk his way through the rest of his life (apparently) but not the first day of shooting. He had to be alert. You didn't hear famous filmmakers saying that their movies fell short of being masterpieces because they'd been sleepy.

He brushed his teeth, washed his face, brushed his teeth again because he was so tired that he'd forgotten he brushed them the first time, and then climbed into bed.

He fell asleep immediately, and if he did dream of ferocious zombies dragging him down into a dark pit, he didn't remember it when he woke up.

Justin woke up exactly one minute before his alarm went off at 5:00 a.m. As far as he could remember, that had never happened in his entire life. Usually his brain was good at plunging into the deepest possible sleep when the buzzer sounded.

He got out of bed and took a shower. He put on a pair of jeans and his favorite *Night of the Living Dead* shirt. (He had four.) Then he looked at himself in the mirror. Wow. He was having a good hair day. It didn't matter since he'd be wearing a baseball cap, but it was still a good omen.

He whistled his favorite song, "The Gonk," as he put on his

socks and shoes. This surprised him because he'd never been able to whistle before. He hoped he wasn't still dreaming.

He poured himself a bowl of Extreme Sugar Flakes, drowned it in milk, and took a bite. Extreme Sugar Flakes had never tasted so good. In fact, milk had never tasted so good, and it hadn't even had time to absorb the natural flavor of the cereal.

This was shaping up to be the most perfect day ever.

He should play the lottery.

No, he didn't have time. And he was a minor.

Still, all signs were pointing to this being the best day of his life. Nothing could spoil it. Nothing! He didn't even care that by constantly thinking about how awesome everything was, he was tempting the forces of irony. Whoever was in charge of irony didn't scare him. This was going to be amazing.

The first location of the day was the park where they'd failed to make *Vampire Tree*. It was only a couple of blocks away from his home, so Justin could walk there. When he was a hugely successful director, he'd take a limousine, even if he was filming in his own driveway, but for now he'd have to be a lowly pedestrian.

Before he went to bed, Justin had put all of his food and equipment in the red wagon he'd gotten for his sixth birthday. It was not the most glamorous way to transport materials. But he only had his learner's permit, and Mom and/or Dad were not inclined to get up this early on their days off to drive him two blocks.

Justin was the kind of ambitious person who would choose the most elaborate, complex scene of the entire movie and put it first in the shooting schedule. Fortunately Gabe had overruled him, and the scenes in the park were relatively straightforward.

When he arrived on location, Gabe was already there, setting up lights. (Well, light. They only had one.) Bobby was also there, lying flat on the ground.

"Hi, Gabe," said Justin.

"Hi, Justin."

"Hi, Bobby."

"Hi," said Bobby in a croak.

"Any special reason you're lying there?"

"I'm dying."

"What's wrong?"

"Everything."

"Narrow it down."

"I think I have the flu."

"For real?"

"I've got a sore throat, and I ache all over. My nose is also running, and I can only tell it's you because I've seen you enough times that I recognize you as a blur."

"Do you need to go home?" Justin said, asking it the same way his mother might ask a yes-or-no question where there was truly only one correct answer.

Bobby shook his head. "I don't want to let you down."

"If you're really sick, you can leave. It's okay," Justin lied.

"No, I'll power through it. Just let me know if you need me to stand up for anything."

Okay, so it was possible that the first day of shooting might not be flawless from beginning to end, but as long as Bobby could stand upright and not drop the boom mic on somebody's head during a take, they'd be fine.

He pulled the wagon over to the park's one picnic table and began to set out the sandwiches, cookies, and water.

"Can I have a cookie?" Bobby asked.

"No. Cookies are for healthy people."

They didn't have an official production designer, but there was no production design necessary for this particular scene since it took place at a regular park and did not require anything to be on fire in the background. Alicia and Christopher were the only two actors in this scene, and they'd been given a 6:30 a.m. call time, so Justin still had half an hour to make sure everything was ready.

"Did you bring everything?" Gabe asked.

"Yep."

"Camera?"

"Yep."

"Extra batteries?"

"Yep."

"Battery charger?"

"We don't have anything to plug it into, but yep."

"Slate?"

"Yep."

"Bribe money?"

"Yep."

"Clown shoes?"

"Those aren't for the park scene."

Gabe glanced at the clipboard he was holding. "You're right. Prop rifle?"

"Yep."

"You should say check instead of yep."

"Do we need to start over?"

"No."

"Good."

"Green bedsheet?"

"Check."

"Clothespins?"

"Check."

"Laptop computer?"

"Check."

"Browsing history deleted?"

"Check."

"Waffle iron?"

"Check."

"Tape measure?"

"Uh-oh."

"It's okay," said Gabe. "I've got three."

"Why do you have three?"

"People like to walk off with tape measures."

"Oh."

"Squirrel food?"

"Why do we need that?"

"In case squirrels swarm us. We discussed this, Justin."

"If squirrels swarm us, we'll break up one of the sandwiches and throw it."

"If squirrels swarm us, it'll be because we have sandwiches lying out. We spent, like, twenty minutes working out this contingency plan."

"Okay, we'll just have to go into filming unprepared. If squirrels force us to cancel, you can punch me in the face. But not hard. Maybe not in the face. You can punch me in the stomach. Also not hard. Actually, having to cancel the shoot will be punishment enough. Don't punch me."

"Clipboard?"

"You're holding one."

"This is mine. You need one for you," said Gabe.

"I'll just use the back of my arm."

"Release forms?"

"Those were your responsibility."

"I know. I'm getting to my own checklist now."

"I'm going to do something else."

"All right."

"Uuuuuuhhhhhhh," said Bobby.

Justin walked over to him. "Can you really not hold your tongue in your mouth, or are you faking?"

"I'm not faking."

"Are you exaggerating?"

"No."

"Because you fake being sick a lot to get out of school."

"I really don't feel good. I'm not going home though. I'm here until the end. I don't care how much my head aches or how much my nose runs or how much my back stings."

"Your back stings?"

"Yeah."

"That doesn't sound like a flu symptom."

"Maybe I have something worse."

"Did you look at the ground before you lay down?"

Bobby did not immediately respond.

"From where I'm standing, I can see three different anthills. You checked for anthills before you lay down, right?"

"I'm pretty sure I did."

"I think you should probably stand up now."

Bobby reached out his arms, and Justin pulled him to his feet. "Are there any ants on my back?" asked Bobby, spinning around.

Justin didn't have time to do an accurate count, but it looked like there were at least eight million. "Get me something to brush them off with!" he shouted at Gabe. "An ant brusher-offer! Hurry!"

"It's not on the checklist!"

"Anything! Hurry!"

Gabe grabbed the green sheet out of Justin's wagon.

"I think they're multiplying!" Bobby wailed.

"They're not multiplying," said Justin, frantically brushing them off with the back of his hand. "There are just a lot of them."

"I think one's a queen and it laid eggs!"

"Stop talking! You're enraging them!"

"One's in my ear! One's in my ear! Now two are in my ear! Now I've got two in one ear and one in the other! Help me!"

Gabe used the sheet to brush the ants off Bobby. "Stop moving!"

"I have to move! I'm panicking!"

"If you keep moving, they'll sting you!"

"I don't want to die! There are still items on my bucket list! I haven't swam in a moat yet!"

"I think I got most of them," said Gabe. "Are there any still in your ears?"

Bobby stuck his fingers in his ears. "I'm not sure. You can't feel stuff crawling on your brain, right? It doesn't have nerves."

"They're not on your brain."

"There are a few in my mouth!" Bobby chewed for a moment and then swallowed.

"Did we get all of them?" asked Gabe.

Bobby scratched under his arms. "I think so. No, wait. There's one squirming around in my belly button." He reached under his shirt and removed the ant. "I hate having an innie."

"Maybe you should go home," said Justin.

Bobby shook his head. "No, overcoming adversity just makes me stronger. I'm all right."

"Your eyes are looking in two different directions."

"No, I'm fine." He took off his shirt. "How many times did they sting me?"

Justin and Gabe inspected his chest and back. "It looks like only twice," said Justin. "That's pretty good for being covered with eight million ants."

"I'm going to lie down some more, if that's okay."

"Maybe pick a different spot."

"I'll lie on the jungle gym."

"There are probably better options."

"The picnic bench?"

"Someplace where you don't get plague germs all over the craft services table."

"My warm bed at home?"

"That might be for the best," said Justin.

"No," said Bobby. "I won't abandon you. You can't make me. I'm just going to go lie on the merry-go-round for a while. Please nobody spin it."

Bobby wandered over to the merry-go-round, and after a couple of unsuccessful attempts, he lay down on it, closed his eyes, and began to softly moan.

"We should call his parents," said Gabe.

"I've seen him look worse," Justin noted. "Let's give him a few minutes to recuperate."

"All right. But if he starts foaming at the mouth, we're calling 911."

"Okay."

"I mean any foam at all. Even if it's just a little bit trickling out of the sides of his mouth. We see any foam, and he's done working for the day."

They heard the putt-putt-putt sound of some sort of motor, and then Christopher came around the corner on a blue moped. Another kid was sitting behind him. Both of them were wearing helmets because Christopher was the kind of upstanding guy who would always be conscious of safety issues when he was operating a motor vehicle, even a tiny one.

He stopped the moped, put out the kickstand with awe-inspiring skill, and got off. He was wearing filthy, torn jeans and a tattered black jacket that perfectly captured the "lost wanderer in a postapocalyptic landscape" look that Justin had asked him to go for.

"Hi, guys," he said with a smile. His teeth were too white for the character, but they'd fix that. "This is my brother. We call him Spork."

The other kid, who looked about twelve, got off the moped.

"You mean, like Spock?" Justin asked.

"Nah. Like the thing that's part spoon and part fork."

"Why do you call him that?"

"Because he hates it."

Spork held up a camera to show them. "Could I watch you guys and get some behind-the-scenes footage? You could use it on the special features reel."

"Yeah, that would be great," said Justin. "Film anything you want."

"Thanks." Spork went over to get some close-up video of Bobby lying on the merry-go-round.

"This is exciting," said Christopher. "I'm really looking

forward to this. Alicia and I got together yesterday to practice our lines, and I think you'll definitely see the chemistry on the big screen."

"That's splendid," said Justin.

14

A MINUTE LATER A CAR ARRIVED, AND ALICIA, WEAR-
ing a tattered white wedding dress, got out of the passenger seat.
The driver was a redheaded girl who was one year older. Justin
recognized her. Her name was Rose or Rosa or Rosalyn or Rosie
or something to that effect.

"Hi, everyone!" the girl said as she got out of the car.

"Hi, Daisy!" said Christopher.

Alicia and Daisy (Justin was close, sort of) walked over to
join them. Alicia had a tiny silver nose ring shaped like a star, and
her hair was now a deep, dark shade of purple like grape Kool-
Aid. It was still, however, down to her shoulders. She held up a
handful of hair and showed it to Justin. "What do you think of
the color?"

"It looks great."

"Is it purple enough?"

"It's very purple."

"My mom literally had a heart attack when she saw it."

"Do you mean *literally* meaning *literally* or *literally* meaning *figuratively*?"

"Literally meaning that she clutched at her chest and fell to her knees and acted like she couldn't catch her breath, but she didn't actually have a heart attack."

"Well, that's a relief. It's not very Mohawky though."

"I know. Daisy was going to cut it for me last night, but she got grounded."

"What'd you do?" Justin asked her.

Daisy shrugged. "There were a lot of things it could've been. I'm not one hundred percent sure which one I was grounded for. My mom said, 'You know what you did,' and I didn't think it was a good idea to confess to something that might have been the wrong thing, y'know."

Justin nodded. "I can relate."

"I know she was going through my closet, but I'm not sure which box she opened."

"Anyway," said Alicia, "she was going to sneak out and cut my hair, and then we decided that we should just do it when we got to the set, so you can make sure it's in line with your vision."

"Thanks," said Justin. "I appreciate that. We're almost ready to roll camera, so you should go ahead and get started."

"Let's do this," said Alicia, pushing her hair away from her left eye.

"Gaaahhh!" Justin said out loud, even though he tried to just think it.

"Oh yeah," said Alicia. "The piercing got infected."

"Doesn't that hurt?"

"It's not as bad as it looks."

"It looks like it's pulsating!"

"It's not pulsating," Alicia assured him. "I put rubbing alcohol on it and did everything you're supposed to do. I'm not sure why it got so bad. Hey, more production value for you, right?"

"Are you sure the pin wasn't rusty? I'm not an expert on eyebrow piercings, but I'm pretty sure it's not supposed to be that color…or that shape…or move like that. Maybe you should take it out."

"Nope," said Alicia. "The truth is that it hurt so bad that I could never do it again, so if I want a pierced eyebrow, this is my only chance. It's okay. Really."

"Your friend just fell off the merry-go-round," said Spork. "Should I help him back on it?"

"Yes, please," said Justin, who was starting to think that things might not go quite as perfectly as he'd believed earlier in the day.

Daisy took an electric razor out of her car, and then she and Alicia walked over to the slide. Alicia sat on the bottom. Daisy crouched down next to her and turned on the razor.

"Breathe," Gabe told Justin. "We're going to get through this."

"I'm breathing fine. My lungs have never worked better."

"Seriously, we're okay. There are bound to be a few hiccups on the first day of shooting."

"If Alicia hiccups, that thing on her eyebrow is going to burst."

"That's gross."

"Yes, it certainly is."

Daisy pushed the razor across the side of Alicia's head. Some purple hair fell to the ground.

"Aaaahhhh!" Alicia cried out. "My hair! My hair!"

"Did you hurt yourself?" Justin asked.

"No!" Alicia ran her fingers over the bare patch. "My hair! Why did I do that? It took me forever to grow my hair that long! What have I done?" She began to cry.

Everybody just stood there for a moment, unsure what to do.

"Ummmm," Justin said.

"I can't believe I let you do that," Alicia said to Daisy. "Why didn't you stop me?"

"You said you wanted a Mohawk!"

"Why didn't you talk me out of it?"

"I thought you really wanted one."

"I did! But not anymore!" Alicia turned her accusing gaze onto Justin. "Why didn't *you* talk me out of it? You're supposed to be the director!"

"I, uh… I, uh… I, uh… I, uh… I, uh…"

"Look at my hair now! I'm hideous!"

"That's not true," said Justin. "If anything is making you hideous, it's the infected eyebrow piercing, not your hair."

Justin took a very brief moment to ponder whether that had been the best possible comment to make at that particular time. He decided that it had not been.

Alicia buried her face in her hands and wept. Spork came over to film her.

"I think if you comb your hair to the side you can cover the bare patch," said Justin, hoping that he was being helpful but suspecting that he wasn't.

Alicia wiped her eyes. "I'm sorry," she said. "I didn't realize I was so attached to my hair."

"It's really not a problem," Justin told her. "There aren't any hair restrictions on the role."

"Maybe in this postapocalyptic future, people shave one piece of the side of their heads. It's just something they do," said Gabe. "If the movie is popular enough, viewers might shave a piece of their heads to be like Veronica Chaos."

"I'm not shaving any of my head," said Christopher. "I'm sorry if it makes me a difficult actor, but that's not what I signed on for. You should have said something during the audition. I'll go purple, but I'm not shaving it."

"Nobody is asking you to shave your head," said Justin.

"But the purple?"

"No."

"I could run home really quick."

"No. There's no reason why everybody's hair would be purple."

"Unless," Gabe said, "the purple dye is what caused the survivors to be immune to the virus that turned everybody else into zombies. That could be the missing piece of the puzzle."

"We're not reworking our mythos now!" said Justin. "Alicia's hair is fine! Christopher's hair is fine! Everybody's hair is fine! We need to get started."

"You know what?" Alicia said. "I think I just freaked out because I'm nervous about being on my first movie set. I want the Mohawk. I really do."

Justin gaped at her. "But you…but you just…but you just said…but you just said that—"

"She does this kind of thing all the time," said Daisy.

"Let's finish this," said Alicia. "I'm ready."

"Wait. No, wait," said Justin. "I mean, we have a lot to shoot today. We don't have time for you to get emotional again."

"Are you calling me emotional because I'm a woman?"

"What? No. You were crying fifteen seconds ago! Your cheeks are still glistening!" Justin couldn't figure out what was happening. Maybe the reason he'd never had a girlfriend was to protect his sanity.

"I'm sorry," said Alicia. "I get defensive when I'm emotional. I'll finish cutting my hair."

"You know what? I'll cut my hair too," said Christopher.

"Your hair is staying exactly the way it is," Justin told him. "Alicia, whatever you decide about your hair is fine with me, but we're going to have to stick with that decision for the rest of the shooting schedule. So I need to know that your heart is prepared to accept whatever happens when the razor starts buzzing."

Alicia nodded. "I'm ready."

Spork pointed his camera at her. "Do you have any final words?"

"Spork, film but don't talk," said Justin.

"Yes, Director."

Daisy turned on the razor again and resumed the task of shaving most of Alicia's head. Alicia trembled as she did it, and a single tear trickled down her cheek, but she remained mostly stoic throughout the process.

"I feel terrible about wasting so much dye on hair that I was going to get rid of," she said.

"There, all done," said Daisy. "You look awesome."

"Do I?"

"Actually, no. Not yet. Nobody show her a mirror until we get some product in there."

Daisy hurried back to her car to retrieve a tube of gel, applied a generous amount to Alicia's hair, and then spiked it up.

"Oh yeah, that looks sweet," said Daisy.

"Yeah, it does," said Justin.

"It sure does," said Christopher.

"Definitely," said Spork.

"You'll be very pleased with the results," said Gabe.

"There's still an ant or two in my ear," said Bobby.

Alicia took out her cell phone, turned on the camera function, and used it to gaze at herself.

Then she burst into tears. She sat there, sobbing for a full minute as everybody tried to pretend that they had something better to watch.

Finally she spoke, "I'm sorry I cried again, but it's just so beautiful!"

"I'm glad you like it," said Justin. "Now I hate to be the bad guy, but the shooting schedule didn't include time for head-shaving and crying, so we really need to get going."

"Aren't you supposed to have a chair that says director on it?" Christopher asked.

"On a bigger-budget production, yes."

"I'll see if I can find one for you."

"Not necessary, but I appreciate it. So here's the scene. Alicia, you're going to—"

"Could you call me Veronica Chaos?" she asked. "I promise I'm not gonna go full method actor on you, but it would be easier for me if you called me by my character's name from now on."

"Oh," said Justin. "Yeah, sure, sure, that's no problem. Veronica, you're going to—"

"Veronica Chaos."

"Excuse me?"

"I don't think she'd ever just go by her first name. It's always Veronica Chaos, never just Veronica."

"That's honestly not how I saw the character."

"Really? I've never thought of her as anything but a 'Veronica Chaos or nothing' type of person. She'd go around and say, 'Call me by my full name, or get a machete to the windpipe!' I'm surprised you didn't see her that way, because that was the first thing that leaped out at me."

"Can we get a ruling, Gabe?" Justin asked.

"It doesn't matter to me," said Gabe. "We're on a really tight schedule, but saying Veronica Chaos doesn't take much longer than saying Veronica, so I think we can spare the extra time."

Justin was not actually concerned about the time that they might lose by pronouncing two extra syllables, but it was a bit early in the process to allow the cast to start dictating the approach to characters that he'd created. It would start with Alicia insisting that she always be called Veronica Chaos, and it might end with the demand that the character communicate entirely by mooing.

"Can we have a brief conference?" Justin asked.

"Sure," said Gabe.

The two of them stepped out of earshot, and then Justin shared his theory about the mooing.

"I agree that we need to keep control," said Gabe. "But in this case I think it's more important to choose our battles. Give her the Veronica Chaos thing, and then when there's a disagreement that actually matters, you can say, 'Do it my way because I bent to your will that other time.'"

"That makes sense."

"Most things I say do."

They rejoined the others. "Yes, we've decided that calling her Veronica Chaos every single time is consistent with the spirit of the character we created ourselves. Thank you for taking the initiative and for understanding our thought process on that issue. Soooooo now let's get to the first scene. You're going to start here." Justin pointed to one side of the park. "And you're going to walk there." Justin pointed to the other side of the park. "By this point, you've killed about seven hundred and fifty zombies, and you're feeling pretty confident about your abilities. You know that it's a world of danger, so you're being cautious because you're not stupid, but you're also pretty sure that this day isn't going to end with you getting eaten by a zombie. So not quite a strut, but you're walking with attitude like you know you're tough. But you also don't think that anybody else is watching, so there's no reason to show off in the way you move. That's how I want you to walk. Does that make sense?"

"Yes," said Alicia.

"Good." Justin turned to Daisy. "Do you want to run slate?"

"Run what?"

Justin picked up the clapboard and wrote on it with a Magic Marker. "It's the person who runs the clapboard. You'll say, '*Dead Skull*, scene 15A, take one,' and then clap the clapper."

"Why do you clap the clapper? I've always wondered that."

"When we're synchronizing the sound to the picture later, the sound of the clapboard gives us an exact point to match them up."

"Makes sense. I'm learning stuff already."

Justin didn't consider himself to be a frequent provider of useful information, so this was nice to hear. "Give me a second to get our sound guy." He hurried over to the merry-go-round. He checked the side of Bobby's mouth for foam and found none. "Hey, Bobby?"

"Monkey?"

"What?"

"Daddy?"

"It's Justin."

"Oh, hello, Justin. I think I'm a little delirious. You're not wearing a hat, right?"

"I am wearing a hat."

"A monkey hat?"

"No."

"Then I'm seeing a different hat."

"We're ready to do the first shot."

"Oh. Okay. I guess I should stop hallucinating and get up then, huh?"

"Yeah."

Bobby sat up. "Whoa! Dizzy spell! Dizzy spell!" He rubbed his forehead. "Aw, jeez, I feel like I've got an ice cream headache without the reward of getting to eat ice cream first."

"Are you going to be able to do this, or should I get an ambulance?"

"Can you keep an ambulance on standby?"

Justin shook his head. "Not in the budget."

"Give me a moment." Bobby glanced around the park. "Alicia's hair looks that way in reality, right?"

"Yes."

"My mind is on the right track then. Let's go make a movie."

Justin and Bobby walked back to join the others. Justin wished that Bobby was wobbling a little less, but at least he was upright.

"Does everybody understand what we're doing?" Justin asked.

Everybody nodded.

Justin felt a sudden tingle of excitement. This was it. The first shot of his first feature film. What could be more historic?

Alicia got in her starting position. Gabe turned on the camera and framed the shot. Bobby held up the boom mic.

"Why do we need a boom mic if I don't have any lines?" Alicia asked.

"I want to capture the natural sound of your footsteps, so we don't have to recreate it later."

"But won't you three be walking right next to me?"

"You can lie down for a while longer, Bobby."

Bobby thanked Justin and returned to the merry-go-round.

"Okay, this is it," said Justin. "Camera ready?"

"Ready."

"Slate."

Daisy stepped in front of the camera. "Scene 15A, take one." She clapped the clapboard without pinching her nose in it and stepped out of the shot.

"Action!"

Alicia began to walk across the park. She was walking exactly how Veronica Chaos would walk. It was perfect! She couldn't have walked more perfectly if her character was entirely computer generated!

Please don't trip. Please don't trip. Please don't trip, Justin thought.

Alicia did not trip. She walked beautifully across the park, walking with attitude but caution until she reached the other side.

"Cut!" said Justin. He was so elated that he almost wanted to cry, though he didn't because there had already been more than enough crying on his set. "That was exactly what I wanted! Gabe, was it in focus?"

"Completely."

"Yes! Then we have our first shot of the movie!" This was what filmmaking was all about! Justin felt invincible. He felt as if he could film a million shots of a million actresses walking across a million parks.

15

"DO YOU WANT ANOTHER TAKE?" ALICIA ASKED.

"Nope, we're good." Justin understood the value of doing multiple takes during the moviemaking process, but they were trying to shoot an entire feature film very, very quickly. So in a best-case scenario, he'd only have to do a second take if a sinkhole swallowed the entire crew on the first.

"Next is your close-up," Justin told Alicia. "You're going to stop, listen, and then say, 'Hello?' If another word feels more natural than hello, go ahead and say it. Just say something that's along the same lines as hello. We're not locking anybody into the written page here."

"Hello will be fine," said Alicia.

Justin took the clapboard from Daisy, rubbed out 15A with his thumb, and wrote 15B in its place. He supposed that he could have just rubbed out the "A" and replaced it with a "B," but he'd remember that for the next shot. He retrieved Bobby, who put on his headphones and picked up his boom mic, and then everybody got in their places for the next shot.

"Action!"

Alicia stopped. She stopped *exactly* the way Veronica Chaos would stop.

She listened. Again, if you hooked Justin's brain to a video monitor and played the mental footage of how Veronica Chaos would walk, this was it.

"Hello?" she said. Perfect. Absolutely perfect. And Justin was glad she'd stuck with the word hello instead of ad-libbing a replacement.

Justin glanced at Gabe. Through the viewfinder, Justin could see that the boom mic was now in the shot.

Actually the boom mic was in motion.

He looked over at Bobby, whose eyes had rolled up in his head. Not all the way like he was possessed by a demon, but enough, and the boom mic slipped out of his hands.

It struck Alicia in the upper left temple, which was exactly where her infected eyebrow piercing was located. The microphone thumped off it and fell to the ground.

If you were to imagine the quietest scream in the world, this would be the opposite.

It was a scream that in the middle of a real zombie apocalypse, would send every zombie for fifty miles scurrying away, deciding that no amount of human flesh was worth the risk. It was a scream that old sailors might discuss in hushed tones on the night of the full moon when they were sharing tales of times they'd experienced genuine fear.

Alicia's immediate shocked response was to clutch her eyebrow in her hand, which even she would have to admit was not the best possible reaction. So she quickly followed her "boom mic smacked into my infected eyebrow" scream with a "my hand smacked into my infected eyebrow" scream, which wasn't quite as loud but certainly wasn't muted.

Bobby, it should be noted, was wearing headphones for the purpose of hearing sounds that were amplified through the microphone, which was on its most sensitive setting. Though Alicia did not scream directly into the boom mic, the noise was louder for him than it was for everybody else, and it was pretty darn loud for everybody else.

Justin rushed forward to try to help his lead actress, but she waved him away. "Leave me alone! Don't touch me! Ow! Ow! Ow!"

Justin tried to remember if aspirin had been included on the checklist. He didn't think it had.

Alicia closed her eyes and took some long, slow, deep breaths.

"I'm sorry," said Bobby.

She charged at Bobby like a wild animal, knocking him to the ground. She picked up the boom mic and began to smack him with it over and over. "How do you like that? Huh? How does that feel?"

Bobby screamed in pain both from the impact of the microphone and from the fact that he was still wearing the headphones.

"Does that feel good? Does it?" *Whack! Whack! Whack!*

"Somebody should pull her off of him," Daisy suggested.

"I'm not comfortable doing that," said Justin.

Whack! Whack! Whack! Whack! Whack!

"I surrender!" Bobby shouted. "I surrender!"

With one last boom mic smack between the eyes, Alicia got up. She paced around, breathing deeply, with her hand placed very gently over her eyebrow.

Spork, who had filmed everything, moved his camera back and forth between Alicia pacing and Bobby lying stunned on the ground.

Justin felt like now was probably a good time to do something, though he was a bit nervous about meeting Bobby's fate. "So, uh, Alicia—"

"*Veronica Chaos!*"

"So, uh, Veronica, uh, Chaos, is it okay if we help our sound guy up, or was the plan to knock him down again?"

"You can help him up."

Gabe and Christopher helped Bobby to his feet. Surprisingly he was not crying, although he had the wide-eyed, shocked look of somebody who'd just survived a plane crash.

"Do you need to go to the hospital?" Justin asked Alicia.

She shook her head. "I just need a few minutes to calm down."

"I wouldn't mind going to the hospital," said Bobby.

Spork pointed the camera at Justin. "So Justin Hollow, director of *Dead Skull*, now that you've had your first on-set battle, how do you feel?"

"I'd rather not talk about it."

"You have to talk about it. I'm recording you."

Justin looked at the camera. "I regret that Bobby didn't have a better grip on the boom mic. As the director, I'm responsible for every element of what happens on the movie set, so I have to shoulder my share of the blame for the incident. I also regret Veronica Chaos's reaction, which I'm sure was not intended to be quite as violent as it ultimately ended up being and which I'm sure was done because of the pain and not because of any sort of personal dispute with Bobby."

"You should put it in the movie," said Spork.

"I'm not going to put it in the movie."

"For what it's worth," said Gabe, "I think we got the shot we needed before Bobby dropped the boom mic on her infected eyebrow, so we won't have to redo it."

Alicia continued to pace, muttering unsettling things under her breath.

"You know," said Bobby, rubbing one of the eighteen places where he'd been hit, "I actually feel better now. I think she knocked the flu out of me."

"I'm pretty sure that isn't medically possible," said Justin.

"My head is clear. It hurts from all the bruises, but I can think straight again. You don't look like Snoopy anymore. I'm ready to make this movie."

"I want him fired," said Alicia.

Justin blinked. "Excuse me?"

"Fire him. Right now."

"I'm not firing him."

"Do it. Be a man."

"Since we all just watched Bobby get beat up by a girl, I'm not sure that 'be a man' is appropriate."

"Fire him, or I will."

Justin glanced over at Gabe as if he was trying to figure out if Alicia had the authority to fire a member of their crew. Then he glanced away from Gabe. Of course she didn't. He was the director. He made all decisions regarding hiring and/or firing. Yes, some sort of disciplinary action was appropriate, but he wasn't going to fire one of his two best friends.

"I'm not doing it," said Justin.

"Fine." Alicia pointed to Bobby. "You're fired."

"No, you're not," Justin told Bobby. "That doesn't count."

"Yes, it does," said Alicia. "Pack up your gear and leave."

Bobby looked unsure of what to do.

"Look, I understand that we've had a very intense few minutes," said Justin. "But nobody is fired. We can work this out between us. Bobby, you're sorry for what you did, right?"

Bobby nodded. "Very much so."

"Veronica Chaos, if Bobby has admitted that he was wrong and promises never to do it again, isn't that enough?"

"No, I want him fired. Or blood. One of the two."

"You can't have either. We are all sympathetic to how you're feeling. If I got my eyebrow pierced, which I never would, but if I did and it got all red and yellow and swollen, the last thing I would want is for something to smack into it. We understand your thirst for vengeance. But without a sound guy, we don't have a movie, and without a movie, your excruciating agony was for nothing."

"You don't have a movie without a star either," Alicia pointed out.

Daisy raised her hand. "I'll play Veronica Chaos if she doesn't want to."

"Traitor!"

"Everybody, please calm down," said Justin.

"No, no, everybody go nuts," said Spork, moving the camera between Alicia and Daisy. "I'm getting great footage."

"Spork, stop trying to manipulate reality," said Christopher. "We discussed this before we got here."

"We're all a team," said Justin. "It's fine if we're dysfunctional. That's what moviemaking is all about. But we have to stick together. Veronica Chaos, you're the perfect Veronica Chaos. Bobby, you're the perfect sound guy…despite the evidence we've seen today. We have to think about what's best for the movie, and losing either one of you is bad for the movie. I know that with the passion that's burning deep in our hearts, we can put this behind us."

"Fire him," said Alicia.

"No," said Justin.

"All right. But if anything like that happens again, I will *end* him. I mean it. He'll be nothing but microscopic traces in the city's water supply."

"Noted," said Bobby.

Justin considered asking the two of them to shake hands, but he was worried that Alicia might crush the bones in Bobby's fingers. Still, nobody had quit or been fired, so Justin was going to consider this a victory.

"Everybody take a five-minute cookie break," he said. "Gabe and I will set up the next shot."

While Bobby, Alicia, Christopher, Spork, and Daisy walked over to the picnic table, a minivan pulled up next to Daisy's car. The doors opened, and several screaming children got out followed by a man and woman. The children immediately began to run around the park, yelling and laughing rather than creating a background that was consistent with a postapocalyptic wasteland.

"Hi," Justin said as he walked over to the adults. "I'm Justin Hollow, and I'm making a feature film."

"Oh, how exciting," said the woman.

"So we need the park."

"All to yourself?"

"If that's all right, yes."

"We're having Hugo's birthday party here. Surely you didn't think that this park would be empty all day?"

"No, not all day, just for the morning. That's why we got here so early."

"Oh, well, Hugo wanted to start his birthday party as soon as possible. My little sweetheart gets so hyper sometimes. Here, Hugo, have some taffy."

Justin noticed that the children were helping themselves to

the cookies. "Hey," he called out. "Those are for cast and crew only." The children, hearing his message, limited themselves to four each.

"Isn't there another park where you could shoot your little movie?" asked the woman.

"Well, we've already done a couple of scenes here, so if we move, our footage won't match. And we were here first."

Hugo, who was very wide, held out his hand. The woman put a candy bar in it. The cast and crew returned with their cookies.

"What kind of movie is it?" asked the woman.

Justin quickly tried to think of an answer that was not "a zombie movie."

"A zombie movie," said Christopher.

The woman scowled. "You should spend a little less time thinking about zombies and a little more time thinking about the Lord."

"Zombies don't exist," said the man. "Why don't you make a war movie?"

"We're not trying to ruin anybody's birthday," Justin insisted. "All we need to do is get a few more scenes done, and we'll be out of your way."

"Zombies," the woman muttered. "You should all be ashamed of yourselves. It's not natural for kids to be into all of that blood and slime. When I was your age, I liked dolls and math."

"Why don't you make a comedy?" suggested the man. "You could film a kid falling off the teeter-totter."

"Zombies are not appropriate subject matter for your age-group," the woman informed Justin. "Do your parents know?"

"Yes, ma'am."

"Do they approve?"

"They know."

"I will not be moving Hugo's birthday party so you cultists can play zombie games." She gave Hugo a handful of gumdrops. "Disgraceful and disgusting."

"Good makeup effects though," said the man, gesturing to Alicia's forehead. "I'll give them that."

"That's not makeup," said Alicia. "It's the snakes in my head trying to get out. If you hold your hand there long enough, you might feel a fang."

"In my day, kids were not smart-alecky to adults," said the woman. "And we didn't do that to our hair."

"This isn't dye. Don't drink the water, or the same thing could happen to you."

The woman handed Hugo a pretzel stick, which he tossed onto the ground. "I think we're done talking to you. We can share the park."

"You should make a movie about cats," said the man.

Another car pulled up next to the minivan. The children squealed with excitement.

"The clown is here! The clown is here!"

16

"HI, EVERYBODY!" THE CLOWN SAID AS HE GOT out of the car. "I'm Stinky the Clown!" He honked a bicycle horn and waved to the children. He walked over to the gathering, moving slowly because of his cartoonishly oversized shiny red shoes.

"Is it safe to drive when you're wearing those?" Gabe asked.

"The judge says yes."

"Don't talk to our clown," said the woman.

While the children gathered around Stinky, Justin waved for everybody on his crew to join him. "This is not an ideal situation," he admitted. "But we're just going to have to work through it. Pretend they're not there."

"I'm going to have trouble ignoring Stinky," said Daisy. "What kind of clown wears pastel? His colors are all muted when they should be vibrant."

"These scenes are where most of the character development happens," said Justin. "So I need everybody to bring their A-game, even with the distractions. If the audience doesn't get to know Veronica Chaos and Runson Mudd as human beings, they won't care when they throw a zombie into an electrified Jacuzzi."

"We couldn't get the Jacuzzi," said Gabe.

"Okay, they won't care when they shove a zombie's head into a microwave."

"I thought we decided that the zombie-head-in-a-microwave bit interrupted the flow of the scene."

"Okay, they won't care when they express emotion."

"I'm ready," said Christopher. "No clown is going to keep me from connecting with the audience."

"Then let's do it!"

"My name is Veronica Chaos," said Alicia.

"I'm Runson Mudd," said Christopher, reaching out his hand. "Nice to meet you."

"Cut!" said Justin. "A kid ran into the shot."

"My name is Veronica Chaos," said Alicia.

"I'm Runson Mudd," said Christopher, reaching out his hand. "Nice to meet you."

"Cut!" said Justin. "Another kid ran into the shot."

"My name is Veronica Chaos," said Alicia.

"I'm Runson Mudd," said Christopher, reaching out his hand. "Nice to meet you."

"Cut!" said Justin. "Hugo! Can't you play someplace else?"

Hugo bit the ear off his chocolate bunny. "It's my birthday. Happy birthday to me!"

"My name is Veronica Chaos," said Alicia.

"I'm Runson Mudd," said Christopher, reaching out his hand. "Nice to meet you."

"Hi, I'm Stinky the Clown!" said Stinky the Clown, leaning into the shot and waving to the camera.

"Cut!" said Justin. "Stinky! C'mon, dude, that wasn't cool."

"I smell like dead fish! Wawawawawa!"

"My name is Veronica Chaos," said Alicia.

"I'm Runson Mudd," said Christopher, reaching out his hand. "Nice to meet you."

Stinky the Clown did a cartwheel in the background. The children chased after him, giggling.

"Seriously, Stinky! Knock it off!" Justin threw half of a cookie at the clown.

"I'm Stinky the Clown! Gabagabagabagaba! I have a pet turtle named Barf! Woowoowoowoowoo! I can eat three hundred pistachios in a weekend! Durdurdurdurdurdur!"

"We have to do something about that clown," said Gabe. "Thirty-eight takes is too many."

Justin walked over to where Hugo's parents sat, carefully pouring sugar into pieces of licorice. "What's it going to take for you to call off the clown sabotage?"

"I don't know what you're talking about," said the woman.

"The sooner we get our shots done, the sooner we leave. By messing things up for us, you're just keeping us around longer."

"Clowns exist to bring happiness to the world. Clowns put smiles on the faces of children. Zombies put frowns on their faces. I don't know about you, but when I look out at the world, I'd rather see smiles than frowns."

"Please make Stinky stop."

"I'm Stinky the Clown!" Stinky announced. "I smell like tapioca pudding you forgot to eat! Zuhzuhzuhzuhzuh! Thubthubthubthub! Gurkle gurkle gonkle gonkle blerp."

"Stinky was hired to entertain these children," said the woman. "If that inconveniences you, that's not our problem."

"I'm Stinky the Clown! The dentist says I don't floss enough! Hargahargahargaharga bock wonk!"

"You have the power to make him stop," said Justin. "Show some compassion."

"Maybe you should show some compassion to Stinky. He's had a rough go of it these past few years."

"I'm Stinky the Clown! Soap is for the weak! Fa fa durken wa!" Stinky honked his bicycle horn and then broke a bottle over his own head.

"If you call off the clown, I'll give you twenty bucks."

"Done," said the woman.

"Really?"

"All we wanted was a simple bribe. Can't you read between the lines?" The woman stood up. "Stinky! You're done for the day. Get back in your cage!"

Stinky hung his head and sadly walked back to his car.

"What's the deal with that?" Justin asked. "Does he think his car is a cage? Is he driving back to a cage? What?"

"Are you here to make a movie, or are you here to ask questions about the clown's backstory?"

"Some things you're better off not knowing," said the man. "Some knowledge leaves you forever haunted."

"My imagination is going to come up with something much worse for Stinky than whatever the truth is," said Justin.

"No," said the man. "No, it is not."

Justin took out his wallet and handed the woman a twenty-dollar bill. "Thanks for your cooperation."

"My name is Veronica Chaos," said Alicia.

"I'm Runson Mudd," said Christopher. "Nice to meet you."

"Cut!" said Justin. "You forgot to put out your hand."

"My name is Veronica Chaos," said Alicia.

"I'm Runson Mudd," said Christopher, reaching out his hand. "Nice to meet you."

Alicia shook his hand.

"Cut!" said Justin.

Alicia sighed. "What was wrong this time?"

"Nothing. That's where we were supposed to cut. On to the next scene!"

For two people who'd never acted in a movie before, Alicia and Christopher were delivering fantastic performances. They were both naturals. No matter what the reviewers might say about his movie ("This movie sucks!"), he didn't see how anybody could criticize their acting.

Justin could not be more pleased.

If he had one tiny little minor detail that he wished he could tweak, it was that they were a tiny little wee bit too convincing about falling in love. He didn't like the way that Veronica Chaos and Runson Mudd looked at each other like they were thinking, *Oh yeah, baby, you're so awesome*, and stuff.

As the director, he knew it would be unprofessional and detrimental to the film to try to make suggestions to fine-tune the lovey looks out of their performances. As a guy who still had a crush on Alicia despite today's discovery that she was crazy, he kind of wanted their onscreen romance to seem less believable.

If he said, "Hey, could you try not to look so much like you're falling in love?" Gabe would call him out on it. He had to think of the movie. The movie came first. If Alicia and Christopher got so immersed in their roles that they just threw their arms around each other and went into a frenzy of noisy smooching,

Justin would not try to pry them apart with a crowbar. It was all about the movie. Nothing else mattered.

While they were setting up the next shot, Gabe glanced around to make sure that nobody was too close and whispered, "What would you think if I asked out Daisy?"

"Huh?"

"Daisy. The girl who's doing the clapboard."

"I know who you mean. You like her?"

"Did you *see* the way she claps the clapboard? She's amazing."

"Until the movie is finished, your relationship needs to stay strictly business. I can't have you complicating things right now. When the movie is done, then you can ask her out."

"When the movie is done, I'm going to Indiana."

"She'll still be here when you get back."

"Is it because you want to ask her out yourself?"

"No!"

"Are you sure?"

"Yes, I'm sure. Why would I do something like that?"

"You saw her use the clapboard too."

"I don't even know what that's supposed to mean. Look, Gabe, I'm not trying to horn in on your action. But as you may have noticed, we're having challenges this morning, and what if she laughs in your face? It will be awkward for everyone."

"I suppose you think she'll laugh in my face but not in yours? What makes your face so great? Huh, Justin? What makes your face so great?"

"You're acting wacky," Justin noted.

"I'm acting wacky because I've suddenly discovered my inner courage and you're trying to shut me down."

"Oh. Wow. I'm sorry. I didn't realize this was an inner courage conversation." Justin patted his friend on the shoulder. "If you want to ask her out, you go right ahead. Just do it quickly because we're really behind schedule."

Gabe nodded and then walked to the other side of the park to talk to Daisy. They spoke for a moment, and then Gabe returned to Justin, looking disheartened.

"She only dates directors."

"Oh."

"So I guess it's safe to make your move."

"I'm not making any move."

"You might as well."

"I have no interest in Daisy."

"Yeah, I'm sure."

"I don't!"

"I saw the way you were looking at her."

"How? With my retinas? How else am I supposed to look at her? Did you forget how I feel about you-know-who?"

Gabe glanced over at Alicia. "Still?"

"Yes!"

"Seriously?"

"Yes!"

"She's kind of a nutcase."

"I know. I don't care."

"You should probably care a little. It's useful information."

"It doesn't matter right now because unlike one of us, I'm here to make a movie, not a baby."

"You're right. You're right," said Gabe. "I apologize. I don't know what came over me. I think it's just because normally in this situation I'd be cowardly, so when I realized that I had the potential to not be a total wuss, I felt like I should act upon it."

"Totally understandable."

"Did Spork get the whole thing on video?"

"Of course."

"Oh well. I'll laugh about it when I'm ninety and dead."

17

"SHOULD I TEXT THE ACTORS FOR THIS AFTERNOON
and postpone their call time?" Gabe asked Justin.

"How far behind are we?"

"Three hours."

Justin massaged his forehead. "How are we going to get back on schedule?"

"Not having more disasters might help."

"Postpone it by one hour. I want to keep moving forward. We'll just try to get Alicia and Christopher's stuff in longer takes instead of setting up so many shots."

"All right." Gabe began to send the texts.

"Okay," said Justin to Alicia and Christopher, "you've been doing a great job so far. I can't promise that you'll both become movie stars, but I guarantee that your pictures will be used in memes. We're pretty far behind because of clown interference, so what I most need from you is to *not stop* during these next few scenes. Stay in character. If you forget your line, make up a different line. If you trip and fall, trip and fall like your character would. We'll fix it in the edit."

"Understood," said Alicia.

"Can we have a quick private discussion?" Gabe asked.

"We just had one."

"This is about something different."

"Okay." Justin and Gabe walked over to the teeter-totter, though they did not do any teeter-tottering while they were there. "What's up now?"

"Are we still trying to make the greatest zombie movie ever?"

"Yes."

"Are you sure? Because comments like 'If you trip and fall, trip and fall in character' feel like there might be some compromising of our creative vision."

"I don't need this now, Gabe."

"No, no, no, I'm not trying to be negative. I'm making sure we're on the same page. If our goal is still to make the greatest zombie movie ever, I'm going to offer different feedback than if we've revised our mission statement to make just a pretty good zombie movie."

Justin thought about that for a while. "Okay, we're going to make the greatest zombie movie ever that was shot on weekends in a month for almost no money. I think we can still accomplish that."

"I agree."

"So maybe we won't make the next *Night of the Living Dead*. Either way, we're going to finish this movie, and it's going to be entertaining enough that nobody involved will be embarrassed by the final product. That's our goal—lack of embarrassment."

"Awesome. Let's do it."

Everybody got in their places.

"Action!"

Alicia and Christopher began their dialogue scene. Christopher immediately scooted closer to Alicia, which technically wasn't in character because at this point in their relationship, Runson Mudd would still be worried that Veronica Chaos might rip off most of his lower jaw. Justin didn't call, "Cut!" though. They had to keep moving. Maybe in postproduction he'd digitally add a few inches of space between them.

Bobby was doing a good job with the boom mic. Three different people had independently made jokes about supergluing the pole to his hands, and though they were all clearly kidding, the serious message behind the humor was not lost on Bobby.

As always, Gabe was flawless with the camera work. The actors were perfectly framed and in focus. Everything was going smoothly. They were going to make up the lost time. The only possible little glitch that Justin could see was that a great big fire ant was crawling on Gabe's neck, but Justin hoped Gabe wouldn't notice until the shot was through.

Gabe's eyes darted downward. He couldn't see his own neck, but he knew something was crawling on it.

But Gabe was a master cinematographer, and no ant crawling on his body was going to distract him from his craft. Though he was twitching a bit, he maintained his concentration on the task at hand.

Justin considered reaching over and brushing it off, but that might be more distracting. As long as the ant didn't sting Gabe, it was no big deal. An entire army of ants had been swarming on Bobby, and only two of them had stung him, so the odds were very much in favor of this ant not feeling any particular reason to sting anybody. Why would it? Gabe had done nothing to hurt the ant or its kind, so unless it had vowed revenge against all of humanity for that one time that Bobby lay on an anthill, there was no reason for concern.

Justin realized that he was watching the ant instead of the performance of his actors, which was not the mark of a good director. He ignored the ant and returned his attention to Alicia and Christopher.

"Your hair is the most beautiful shade of lavender I've ever seen," said Christopher.

"It's not lavender," said Alicia.

This was nowhere close to any dialogue that appeared anywhere in the script. Justin had encouraged their artistic freedom, but only when they weren't saying dumb things. He pointed to his hair and shook his head, hoping that it conveyed the message, "This dialogue is lame. Say other dialogue."

"It *is* lavender," said Christopher. "To me, it's lavender. We're in a whole new world now, Veronica Chaos, and in this world we get to make up our own colors."

I should probably say, "Cut!" now, thought Justin.

No. He'd give them a chance to get back on track. Real people said idiotic things all the time, as evidenced by several of the conversations he'd had this very morning. This might give his movie an element of realism that was lacking from other films in the genre.

"Then what color are my eyes?" asked Alicia.

"They're lavender."

"But they don't match my hair."

"Don't you see? They don't *need* to match your hair. In this new world, all colors can be lavender if we want them to be. That tree over there? It's lavender. When we chop the head off a zombie, a glorious lavender spray of blood comes out. It's an entire universe of lavender."

"That's really, really stupid," said Alicia.

"Yes, it is," Christopher agreed, "but isn't it wonderful that we have the power to control how stupid the world is? Before, other people were in charge of stupidity, but not anymore! Not anymore!"

Yep, better call, "Cut!", thought Justin.

The ant had now crawled up onto Gabe's cheek. He was trying to ignore it, but a thin trickle of sweat was running down his forehead. Justin reached over and brushed the ant off his face.

The ant dropped onto Gabe's neck and then crawled under his shirt collar.

Gabe yelped in pain.

He dropped the camera onto the grass.

Or to be more specific, he dropped the camera onto a rock that rested on the grass.

Justin was sure that the sound of the *crack* did not actually echo. It was all in his mind.

He crouched down and picked up the camera. Much of it, at least eighty percent, was in fine shape. No damage whatsoever. If you ignored the fact that the lens was completely shattered, dropping it onto a rock hadn't been bad at all.

Everybody was very, very silent.

Justin stood up. He tried to turn the camera back on. The only thing that happened was that the bottom of it dropped off, landing on the rock.

Everybody continued to be very, very silent.

Justin picked up the other half of the camera and cradled both halves to his chest like it was an infant.

"The ant went down my shirt and stung me," Gabe explained.

"I know."

"Are you mad?"

Justin shook his head. "No."

"It's okay if you are."

"I'm not mad."

"How are you feeling?"

"A little numb."

"Maybe that is for the best."

"I also kind of feel like I want to start cackling with laughter. You know, when you just sit in the corner and you rock back and forth and you hug yourself and you just laugh and laugh and laugh and you can't stop? That kind of scary, high-pitched laugh."

"Like the Joker?"

"Way crazier than that."

"If you need to do that, go ahead. We've all been there."

"Nah. It's sufficient that I'm doing it in my mind."

"Let us know when you're done."

"I will."

Everybody went back to being very, very silent. Finally Bobby said, "This is worse than when I dropped the boom mic, right?"

"Not now, Bobby," said Gabe.

"Really? I thought the question was perfectly timed." Bobby glanced around at everybody else as if he was trying to see if they agreed with him, but nobody spoke.

"One," said Justin.

"What?" asked Gabe.

"One."

"One what?"

"One rock. As far as I can tell, there is only one rock on the ground in this entire park. Everything else is soft grass. Soft, fluffy grass. If the camera had dropped literally anyplace else on the ground, it probably would have bounced right back up into your hand. One rock. Just one."

"How badly is it damaged?" asked Alicia.

Justin shook the camera. Several pieces fell out.

"You have another one, don't you?"

"No."

"Can you borrow Spork's?"

Spork shook his head. "My dad said to not let anybody else touch it."

"Can you buy another one?" Alicia asked Justin.

"We didn't budget for a new camera."

"Can you get it fixed?"

"I don't know."

"Can you rent one from somewhere?"

"Maybe."

"Are you still laughing in your mind?"

"No. Now it's this black void."

"We can't let this stop us," said Bobby. "We've got too many sandwiches left."

"This isn't the end," said Justin. "All I need is five minutes to have a complete meltdown. When I'm done, I'll come up with a solution, and we'll move forward. Daisy, may I borrow your car for my meltdown?"

"Are you going to break any windows?"

"No."

"Are you going to rip the upholstery?"

"There won't be any destruction."

"Will you practice proper bladder control?"

"Yes."

"All right. It's unlocked."

Justin walked over to Daisy's car, opened the door, climbed into the front seat, shut the door, checked to make sure that all of the windows were closed all the way, and then let out a loud, long bellow.

It was the loudest and longest bellow of his entire life. He was not typically one to indulge in bellowing, so it wasn't as if there was much to compare it to, but this was twice as loud and at least three times as long as any previous bellow he could remember.

He was pretty sure that everyone could still hear it, but he didn't care.

He bellowed and yelled and screamed and cursed and shouted and hollered and accidentally yodeled and coughed, but he didn't cry. His tear ducts were too manly for that.

"AAAAAAAAAARRRRRRRRRRRRRRRGH!!!!"

He should have set a timer so he knew when to conclude his meltdown. Oh well. He'd estimate it.

"AAAAAAAAAARRRRRRRRRRRRRRRGH!!!!"

He wished he hadn't promised not to destroy the upholstery. Gnawing on the seats would help relieve some stress.

Justin bellowed for a while longer, but since he was feeling particularly mature, he decided not to go for the whole five minutes. He got out of the car and returned to the cast and crew.

"We don't have time to get a new camera," he said. "If we lose any more time, we'll never catch up. Therefore, we're going to make this movie with our phones."

He looked at Gabe.

"Why are you looking at me?" asked Gabe.

"Because I know you're going to say something."

"I have no comment about that."

"Really?"

"No, not really. I just didn't want to be the first one. But since you put me on the spot…I'll say no. I'm not making this movie on a phone. I don't want people to say that it looks like we shot it with our phone. They'll mean it as an insult."

"It'll be fine…because now we're making a found-footage movie."

"We are?"

"It's the perfect solution. In a found-footage movie, you don't have to worry about good camera work or keeping things in focus or even if people can tell what's happening."

"But those are all elements that improve a movie."

"We'll still have good acting and cool zombies and guts flying everywhere. We'll just pretend that the characters are filming it themselves."

"We didn't write the script to be found footage."

"Yeah, and we didn't write the script to be made with a camera that got dropped on a rock!"

"This whole time I've been the one saying we should scale things back," said Gabe. "I just don't want to scale them back to crap."

"We're finishing this movie."

"This isn't the movie we wanted to make anymore."

"It's the movie *I* still want to make. If you don't like it, you can quit."

"Then I quit." Gabe turned and walked away.

18

"FINE! QUIT, YOU QUITTER! QUITTY MCQUITTERSON!
Go ahead and take all your stuff and go home!"

Gabe stopped walking and turned back. "I'm not taking my
stuff. You're still welcome to use it. Just make sure you return it
when you're done."

"Oh no, we wouldn't want you to worry about your precious
equipment! Let the baby take his ball and go home!"

"No, seriously. You at least need the clapboard, or else the
scenes and takes won't be properly labeled when you're assembling
the footage for editing. It'll be a nightmare trying to figure out
which is which. Also, the light is mine, and you'll need that to
make sure the shots are properly lit. If you're shooting the movie
on a phone, adequate lighting will be more important than ever."

"Fine. We'll borrow your stuff, quitter!"

"If you have any technical questions, just call me or send a text."

"I think we'll be okay without your vast expertise, quitter!"

"And I've worked long enough today that I've earned one of
those peanut butter sandwiches."

"Oh, really?"

"Yes, really."

"Fine, I agree that you're entitled to *one* of those sandwiches. But that's all you get."

"And a cookie."

"People who break cameras don't get cookies."

"I get as many cookies as Bobby did, and I saw him eat at least twelve. If you subtract the two cookies I've already eaten, I get ten."

"No way are you taking ten cookies," said Justin. "I mean it. You can have four, and that's being generous."

"If you think I'm going to walk out of here with only four cookies, you're crazy."

"Well, then clearly you weren't listening when I was screaming in Daisy's car because I've already made it clear that I'm crazy."

"Ten cookies," said Gabe. "I've earned them."

"If you walk away from my craft services table with ten cookies, you're going to have zero fingers to hold them."

"Guys, we're supposed to be a team!" shouted Bobby.

"Shut up, Bobby!" yelled Justin. "If you hadn't eaten so many cookies, then Gabe wouldn't be trying to take so many of them!"

"Don't tell me to shut up."

"I'm sorry. That wasn't cool."

"It's okay."

Gabe walked over to the craft services table and began to take cookies. "One...two...three—"

"You'd better stop at four," Justin warned him.

"Four—"

"That better be where you stop."

Gabe looked at the remaining cookies, bit his lip, and then put back the four he'd taken. "You're right," he said in a quiet voice. "I don't deserve any cookies."

"Oh, sure, you say that after you've already put your grubby hands all over them! Take those four cookies! Nobody wants them now!"

Gabe sadly walked away from the table.

"At least separate them from the others! We don't know which is which!"

"Good luck with your movie," said Gabe.

"Good luck with being a *jerk*! We don't need luck! We have skill! You were the one holding us back! I think that clown hated you the most! So you just go home and suck your thumb or whatever it is that quitting babies do and leave us to make our movie in peace!"

Gabe walked away from the park. Justin wanted to shout additional negative comments at him, but the one about sucking his thumb had been a pretty devastating blow. Plus he didn't want to shout something less brutal that might detract from its impact.

"You wanna quit too?" Justin asked Bobby.

"No, I barely avoided getting fired."

"Anybody else?"

"Nobody wants to quit," said Christopher. "But is this movie really more important than your friendship?"

"Yes."

"Are you sure? Because—and I mean this in the nicest possible way—so far it doesn't feel like a real movie."

"*What...did...you...just...say?*"

"Don't get me wrong. We're all having fun making it. But you guys have been friends for a long time, and I don't think this movie is worth ruining that."

"You're fired," said Justin. "Bobby, you're playing Runson Mudd."

"Sweet," said Bobby.

"Then who's doing sound?" Christopher asked.

"Daisy can do sound. She watched Bobby do it. It's not that hard."

"And who's running the camera?"

"You are."

"You're firing me as the lead actor but hiring me as the cameraman?"

"Yes. No, wait. That's ridiculous. No, you're completely fired from the movie. I'm operating the phone. That's how we should have been doing this in the first place."

Justin hated that he was behaving like a tyrant. But when James Cameron directed a movie, people on the set had nervous breakdowns left and right. His films were all box office smashes, so he was doing something right. Maybe Justin needed to be even more of a tyrant.

"Does anybody have a copy of the script?" asked Bobby. "I need to start learning my lines."

"See ya," said Christopher. "Veronica C., text me when you get off work. We'll go get butterscotch ice cream sundaes."

Christopher began to walk away.

Good. Let him walk away. Maybe he'd trip.

No, Justin didn't really want him to trip. Sprained ankles were extremely painful.

"Wait," Justin called out. "You're unfired. I agree. It doesn't feel like a real movie so far. But that's going to change. I promise."

Christopher shrugged and walked back over. "Is Gabe unfired too?"

"No. He quit. And he can stay quit for all I care. If he wants to come crawling back, begging us for his job, going all, 'Oh, I made a mistake. I don't know what I was thinking. I'm such a dork, dur dur dur!' then I'll consider it. But I'm not making any special effort to get him back."

"It's not really a special effort," said Christopher. "We can still see him. He's right over there."

"Ignore him," said Justin. "This movie will be twenty-five percent better without him." He took his cell phone out of his pocket. "Okay, we're going to have to reshoot everything we've done so far today, but that's fine because this will be a lot easier. You don't have to worry about not looking at the camera anymore. In fact, I *want* you to look at the camera. You know you're being recorded."

"Who's recording us?" asked Alicia.

"We'll figure that out later."

"It's kind of hard to know how to behave in scene if we don't know who's recording us. If my mom has the camera, it's a lot different than if it's the leader of a horde of cannibals."

Justin supposed she was right. Gabe was always good at spur-of-the-moment story changes. If only he was still part of the project.

Maybe Justin should call out to him and try to get help with just this one creative decision.

No! They didn't need Gabe. Gabe was the kind of whiner who was always insisting on plot logic and character motivation. The movie would go much faster without having to worry about that kind of nonsense.

"You're being filmed by Doug," he said. "We'll decide exactly who Doug is later, but he's not hunting you. He's just a regular guy."

"Does Doug talk to us?"

"Doug's vocal cords were melted. We'll add a scene at the very beginning of the movie where that happens. So no, you won't carry on any conversations with Doug. If it feels natural, you can say, 'Hey, look over there, Doug!' or something like that. If you want to ask a yes-or-no question, I can move the camera up and down to nod or left and right to shake Doug's head, but for the most part, just pretend that Doug isn't there."

"Got it," said Alicia.

"Are we going to get screenplay credit for making up so much of the dialogue?" asked Christopher.

"No. Places, everyone!"

"Action!"

Alicia walked across the park.

"Cut!"

"Wasn't I walking right?"

"Sorry, you were fine, but I can see one of the clown's balloons in the sky. We have to wait for it to float out of the frame."

"Action!"

Justin carefully followed Alicia as she walked across the park. He could tell that the scene was going in and out of focus, but that symbolized the way the *world* was going in and out of focus. This wasn't so hard. Gabe's abilities were overrated.

In fact, if it weren't for Gabe, he probably would've finished his first feature film six or seven years ago. Gabe ruined everything.

Stupid Gabe. Movies without Gabe were so much better. Justin should have fired him as a friend the first day they met.

"Cut!" he said. "Perfect!"

He wondered what Gabe was doing now that they couldn't see him anymore. Probably still walking home. Was he pouting? Was he muttering? Was he standing just out of their field of vision, trying to work up the nerve to come back and grovel?

It didn't matter. This was a Gabe-free motion picture. And that was the way all motion pictures should be.

He missed Gabe.

No, he didn't. Gabe was a loser with both an uppercase *and* a lowercase *L*.

Justin didn't need him, and that was final.

It was amazing how quickly the shoot went now that they'd stopped obsessing about quality. Literally every shot was good enough.

And Justin was starting to think that Doug was the true star of the movie. Veronica Chaos and Runson Mudd were just supporting players in the story of Doug. He wouldn't share that with Alicia and Christopher though. He didn't want them to get jealous.

They finished up the scenes in the park, and then it was the special time that everybody had been waiting for.

Time for the zombies!

19

"WHAT'S THAT SMELL?" ALICIA ASKED AS THEY stood on Uncle Clyde's porch.

"It always smells like this," said Bobby.

"Yeah, but what *is* it?"

"I'm not sure," Bobby admitted. "It's definitely not a dead body or anything, so you don't have to worry."

Christopher sniffed. "It smells kind of fruity and kind of deathy."

"I promise it's not death," said Bobby. "He likes to burn candles, and he doesn't always pick the scents that are best for your nose. You'll get used to it."

Bobby knocked on the door.

Nobody answered.

"Are you sure he's home?" Justin asked.

"Of course he's home. He knew we were coming. He wouldn't let us down." Bobby knocked again.

"I think that smell is your uncle's corpse," said Christopher.

"It is not. He wouldn't die right after we gave him money."

"Should we try the doorbell?" asked Justin.

"No, we'd get electrocuted. That's why there's tape over it."

Alicia took a deep whiff. "I can't smell the fruit part."

"It's there," Christopher assured her. "There's a hint of citrus underneath the rot."

"It's not rot," said Bobby.

"We didn't say it was human rot. There could be a dead caribou in there."

Bobby knocked again. "Uncle Clyde? Uncle Clyde?"

"Your uncle is so dead," said Alicia.

"I already told you it smells like this all the time, and every time I've seen Uncle Clyde, he's been alive. He's just so busy working that he can't hear us."

"He's probably drunk and unconscious," said Justin. "When I talked to him, I did get a 'will be drunk and unconscious soon' vibe."

The front door swung open. Everybody immediately gained a new appreciation for the door's role in keeping the smell mostly contained within the house.

It was kind of like if there'd been an Easter egg hunt, but the person in charge had forgotten to hard-boil one of the eggs and hidden it in such a clever spot that none of the children found it on Easter morning, so it just sat there, doing what eggs do when they're left out in the sun—except instead of one egg, it smelled like it was eighty eggs. And when the gardener found the eggs a week later, he cracked them open and poured the ooze into a bucket, the contents of which were flung into everybody's face when Uncle Clyde opened his front door. It was just like that, except only as a smell, not actual eggs.

Uncle Clyde looked like he hadn't slept in three days or showered in twelve. He blinked at them as if unsure if he was seeing humans or aliens, and then apparently satisfied that they weren't aliens (or were at least friendly aliens), he motioned for them to come inside.

Bobby followed. Everybody else looked to Justin, their leader, for guidance. He walked inside as well.

There were a lot of words you could use to describe Uncle Clyde's house. Two of the more polite ones were "small" and "interesting."

Justin was the biggest horror movie fan he knew. Not in a snotty "You don't appreciate the nuances of *Land of the Dead* as I do" manner, but nobody could beat him for sheer enthusiasm. Horror movies were *cool.* Horror movie memorabilia was *cool.* And so Uncle Clyde's house should have been *cool,* but it wasn't *cool.* It was creepy and disturbing.

There wasn't furniture made of bones or chickens locked in small cages or a pile of mostly dead serpents. Nor were there faces on the floor, dolls with cracked faces, or skinned people hanging upside down from the ceiling, whispering, *Help me. Help me. I'll give you fifty bucks if you help me.* There also weren't messages written in blood on the wall, saying how neat the devil was. There weren't half-human and half-fly creatures trapped in spiderwebs or old men sitting in wheelchairs with roadkill in the tires.

And he didn't see any Muppets with their eyes removed, ectoplasm dripping from a piano, carnivorous plants doing musical numbers, people who'd had acid thrown in their faces, people who were just heads, people who were just brains, or people who were just armpits.

There weren't glass tubes of eight-foot-long toenails, scarecrows with a real person inside, a grim reaper's scythe with eighteen blades, a spleen lying around, a matching pair of mummies, a computer without an Internet connection, or a life-sized model of Justin Bieber made entirely of teeth.

It was a perfectly normal living room.

A normal couch. A normal recliner. A normal coffee table. Some normal pictures of normal people hanging on the normal walls. A normal lamp. A normal television. A normal trombone. A shelf that wasn't quite as normal as the other items in the living room but was still pretty darn normal.

Justin couldn't figure out why it was so upsetting. Maybe it was the fact that he didn't know why it was spooky that made it so spooky. Fear of the unknown.

None of the others had run screaming from the house yet, so Justin decided that he should set a good example and not do that either.

"Come on down to the basement," said Uncle Clyde.

"I didn't think any homes in Florida had basements," said Justin.

Uncle Clyde winked. "They're not *supposed* to."

He opened a door and headed down a flight of stairs. Bobby followed him, which seemed to indicate that they were not headed down into a spike-filled pit, so Justin and the others went down the stairs as well.

In the basement were several long tables covered with absolutely nothing. The walls and floor also had nothing. It was a surprisingly empty basement for what was supposed to be a makeup effects lab.

"Where's all the zombie stuff?" Justin asked.

Uncle Clyde gestured to the tables. "You're looking at it."

"There's nothing there."

"Sure there is. Look at those tables. My old tables were all scratched up. You could eat off these."

"This is what you spent the money on?"

"What was I supposed to spend it on?"

"Zombie stuff!"

"Haw haw haw!" Uncle Clyde laughed. His laughter was such that you could actually hear the *h* and *w* sounds in "haw." He laughed and laughed, his belly shaking like a bowl full of custard. It was the kind of laughter that could either mean "I've trapped you down here forever" or "I played an amusing joke." Justin hoped it was the latter.

"I'm just kidding," said Uncle Clyde.

"He likes to kid," said Bobby.

"You should've seen your face."

"He likes to see people's faces after he kids."

"I'll go up and get the zombie stuff. Be right back."

Justin didn't feel particularly safe with that idea, but he decided to avoid the awkward moment and let Uncle Clyde go.

"He does like to kid around," said Bobby. "One time he pretended to pull a quarter out of my ear, and then he told me it was a tumor."

"I can't say that I like your uncle very much," said Justin. "No offense."

"No offense taken. Most people don't."

"I've figured out what the smell is," said Alicia. "It's loneliness."

Uncle Clyde came back down the stairs, holding a cardboard box that was about the size of four heads. He placed it on one of the tables, opened the lid, and took out a mannequin head, upon which was an unbelievably detailed zombie mask.

"Whoa!" said Justin.

"Pretty great, isn't it?"

"It's one of the best zombie masks I've ever seen!"

"When Uncle Clyde promises, Uncle Clyde delivers."

"This is incredible. I'm sorry I..." Justin almost listed some of the unkind thoughts he'd had about Uncle Clyde but then thought better of it. "Let's see the rest of them."

Uncle Clyde raised an eyebrow.

"The rest of them," Justin repeated. He pointed to the box just in case his meaning was unclear. "The rest of the zombie masks that are in that box."

"Rest?"

"You made more than one, right?"

"Not that I recall."

"That's it? That's the only mask you made?"

"Yes. It surprises me that you thought there'd be more."

"Our deal was that you'd make as many zombie masks as possible with the five thousand bucks!"

"And I did exactly that."

"How does one mask cost five thousand dollars?"

"Labor."

Justin wanted to throw an explosive fit, but he also thought it might be a good idea to direct his anger toward somebody besides the creepy guy. "Bobby, you said he could do all of the zombies for our movie!"

Bobby gulped. He looked like he wanted to be anywhere but right here. He licked his lips. Smoothed back his hair. Cleared his throat. "Uncle Clyde," he began, "when I talked to you, you *did* say that you could make all of our zombies, no problem."

"I'm not the one saying there's a problem."

"Right." Bobby gulped again. "What Justin is saying—and I agree with him—is that we were under the impression that we would get more than one zombie for our investment. It's our fault for not locking down an exact number in writing, and we'll know that for future projects. But you do have to admit that you kind of implied that we'd get multiple zombies."

"If that's the implication you inferred, then that's on you," said Uncle Clyde. "A measly five thousand bucks isn't enough to cover the average special effects artist's weekend gambling debt. What did you think you were going to get? *The Avengers vs Zombies*? If you went to Greg Nicotero with a five-grand budget, he'd give you a roundhouse kick to the face."

"Nobody is saying that the budget wasn't an insult," said Bobby. "But you agreed to it."

"Only because you're my nephew. If you were a real person, I would've laughed in your face."

"You laughed in our face when we first came down here," Justin pointed out.

"Stay out of this," Uncle Clyde told him. "It doesn't concern you."

"Huh? It kind of does…I mean…I'm the…I'm responsible for the…uh…never mind."

"I delivered what I promised," said Uncle Clyde. "If you misinterpreted that promise to mean something much less tiny, then that's your own fault."

"Look," said Bobby, "I don't want to play the 'we're only fifteen years old' card, but we're only fifteen. Give us a break. Make us more zombies."

Uncle Clyde furrowed his brow as he considered the request. "I'd have to spend my own money to get more materials. Family or not, that's a pretty big request. I want a possessive credit. I want the film to be called *Uncle Clyde's Death Skull*."

"That's not gonna happen," said Justin.

"Just out of curiosity," said Christopher, "why would you

want it called *Uncle Clyde's Death Skull* instead of your real name? That seems weird. Unless your first name is Uncle and your last name is Clyde, which would be even weirder."

Uncle Clyde ignored him. "Bobby, you're not my favorite nephew, but you're also not my least favorite nephew. I'll make these zombies for you…in exchange for one favor."

"What?"

"I want you to eat a raccoon paw."

"Excuse me?" asked Bobby.

"I've got a raccoon's paw upstairs. I want you to eat it."

"I beg your pardon?"

"The raccoon is fine. Don't worry."

Bobby looked over at Justin for advice. Receiving none, he looked over at Alicia. Receiving none there either, he looked at Christopher and then at Spork. Nobody had any wisdom to impart about the raccoon situation.

"Is the paw, uh, fresh?"

Uncle Clyde nodded. "It's only been in the fridge for a couple of weeks."

"Is it small enough to swallow whole? Or do I have to chew it?"

"There will be some chewing involved."

"Can I have a glass of milk with it?"

"Yes."

"Is there a time limit?"

"No. Actually, on second thought, yes. You have five minutes to get it down. If you go past that, I'll find another raccoon, and you have to eat another one."

"I really don't want to do this," said Bobby.

"And I didn't want to kill a man in prison," said Uncle Clyde. "So I didn't. We have the power to make our own choices."

Bobby looked as if he wanted to start tearing out his hair, but he made the choice not to. "I'll do it," he said. "I'll eat the raccoon paw. I'll chew it if that's what it takes, and I'll even eat the fur and the claws. All I ask is one thing. Please don't let the raccoon watch."

Uncle Clyde laughed and slapped him on the back. "Haw haw haw! I was only kidding. I've got plenty more zombie materials upstairs. I wouldn't swindle a bunch of kids. I only rip off adults. I just want extra screen time in the bonus features on the Blu-ray."

"You'd probably get along really well with my grandmother," said Justin.

Uncle Clyde raised an eyebrow. "Is she hot?"

UNCLE CLYDE SHOWED THEM THE VARIOUS ZOMBIE faces and wounds he'd created, and Justin felt his eyes tear up with emotion at the beauty of it all. Uncle Clyde was a genius. A bizarre genius, yes, but it was okay for geniuses to be weirdos as long as they did cool stuff.

Justin and Bobby set up the green screen (the bedsheet he'd brought with him) against the basement wall. While Uncle Clyde put zombie makeup on the actors, Justin would shoot the scenes that would require them to digitally insert the backgrounds later. Sadly it was impractical to think that they could shoot inside of a volcano or a destroyed city or Iowa.

The doorbell rang. Somebody cried out in pain.

Uncle Clyde hurried upstairs and returned a moment later with Butch Jones, who would be a zombie victim in Iowa. He walked over to Justin, staggering slightly.

"Thanks for being in my movie," said Justin, shaking his hand.

"Anytime. I've always wanted to get killed by a werewolf."

"It's a zombie movie."

"Eh. Same thing."

"I notice that you're wearing a green shirt."

Butch stroked the front of his shirt with pride. "Yep. My favorite shirt. Birthday present from my grandfather before he died. I tore it up just like you wanted."

"But it's green."

"It is. Very green."

"The way a green screen works is that we shoot you against a green screen," Justin said, pointing to the sheet. "Later we combine this footage with different backgrounds. The computer removes everything in your shot that is green and replaces it with images from the background. So technically the only color you could wear that would mess up what we're trying to accomplish here is green."

"Oh."

"That's why I told you that your scenes would be shot against a green screen. I didn't want you to unnecessarily tear up a shirt that your grandfather gave you before he died."

"You're going to reimburse me for the shirt, right?"

"No."

"I think you should. I wouldn't have ripped it up if it weren't for your movie. I'm not destructive."

"I explained the situation."

"No, you didn't. Why would a civilian like me be expected to understand how the process of green screen technology works? Not everybody is a film geek. Some of us just watch movies without understanding how they're made. If I was not provided with a layman's explanation for what we'd be doing today, that's your failing as a director, not mine as a performer."

"How much was the shirt?"

"Twelve bucks."

"Fine."

"Plus two bucks for the sentimental value."

"Fine."

"And I guess I'll need another shirt that's not green."

"Would you be willing to do the scene without a shirt?"

"Absolutely! Why didn't you ask that in the first place?"

They began shooting the many scenes that they needed to finish against the green screen. It went faster than Justin could have ever imagined. Even when Alicia and Christopher messed up the occasional line, it didn't matter. Thanks to the found-footage format, he could just add in some static and edit around the mistake.

Making a movie was *easy*. Why had anybody ever said that it was difficult? He was crossing scene after scene off his list, and even adding plenty of new ones because his cast was so good at improvisation.

The actors walked across the green screen, ran across it, walked toward it, walked away from it, kicked things on it that he'd add later, survived a helicopter crash against it, and on and on. Sure, not everything made sense, but everybody in the business knew that movies were truly created in the editing room.

"Your first zombie is ready," Uncle Clyde announced.

Duane Parker, a sophomore Justin barely knew, strutted over to the green screen. He'd been cast in the pivotal role of Zombie with Inflatable Zebra around Its Waist. *Dead Skull* was still emphatically not a comedy, but if you wanted to be realistic, you had to acknowledge that somebody probably would have died with an inflatable zebra around his waist.

"You're going to be one of our slow zombies," Justin explained. "Do a practice walk for me."

Duane walked across the basement.

"Okay, that's more like a dance."

"I don't feel like I'm dancing."

"Maybe you're not dancing, but you're walking with musical rhythm. Are you thinking of a song?"

"I'm always thinking of a song."

"Well, try walking without a song in your head."

Duane walked across the basement again.

"See, the problem is that you're bouncing a little. You're bobbing your head, and you're snapping your fingers."

"I was snapping my fingers?"

"Yes."

"That's interesting. I didn't realize that about myself."

"So what I'd like you to do is sort of shuffle across the room like a reanimated corpse and not dance like a theater student."

"Will do."

Duane walked across the basement once more.

"Better," said Justin. "Still snapping your fingers though."

"I swear I'm not aware that that's happening."

"It's no big deal. How about when you walk, you look down at your hands, and if you see your fingers starting to snap, you can make them stop?"

Duane walked across the basement for what Justin suspected would not be the last time.

"Okay," said Justin, "the fingers have stopped, but the head-bopping is still very much a thing."

"It's just so strange. I'm surprised that nobody has mentioned this to me before."

"Well, unless they were directing you how to walk like the living dead, it probably wouldn't have come up."

"That makes sense."

"What I want you to do is think of your absolute least favorite song, something you can't dance to, and I want you to sing it in your head while you're walking."

Duane nodded. Then we walked across the basement slowly and sadly with no rhythm.

"Yes!" Another directing challenge overcome! Justin would never suggest that he was one of the ten best directors working today, but he knew he wasn't one of the ten worst either. "Are you ready for your scene?"

Duane scratched at his chin. "Is it bad if my skin feels like it's on fire underneath the latex?"

"Yes, it is actually. Are you having an allergic reaction?"

"Nah. Uncle Clyde told me to say that. He's one amusing dude."

"He certainly is. The first thing I need you to do is just shamble across the green screen. This is the very first scene we're shooting with a zombie in it, so you'll be a trivia question one day."

Duane got into place. Bobby held up the boom mic. Justin pressed Record on his phone camera. Daisy did the clapboard, and Justin said, "Act—"

He stopped before he could finish the word. He lowered his phone.

"Were you telling me to act, or were you starting to sneeze?" asked Duane.

"Neither. Give me a minute."

This was the first shot with a zombie, and Gabe wasn't here. It was wrong.

Gabe was his producer. Gabe was his friend. Yes, he'd dragged

Gabe into this whole project despite his many protests, but this was a movie they were supposed to make *together*.

If Gabe wasn't here, then Justin didn't want to make this movie.

No, wait. Yes, he did. It would be silly to dump it after all the work he'd put in. But he'd much rather make it with Gabe, if at all possible.

"I have to go," he said.

"Where?" asked Bobby.

"To get Gabe."

"You could just call him. You're holding a phone."

Justin shook his head. "That's not the cinematic thing to do." He walked over to the stairs. "Everybody wait for me. Practice your lines and your walk. I'll be right back."

"Can I follow you with the camera?" asked Spork.

"Yes! That's a perfect idea. We'll preserve this moment."

Justin and Spork ran up the stairs and out the front door.

"Gabe!" shouted Justin as he ran down the sidewalk. "Gabe!" They weren't anywhere close to Gabe's house, but since Spork was recording this, Justin felt like he should be yelling his friend's name.

Justin continued running. He was in pretty good shape for a filmmaker, which meant that he was in pretty bad shape. He didn't want Spork to record him slowing down, so he forced himself to keep running. He shouldn't have eaten so many cookies.

"Gabe! Gaaaaaaabe!"

"Yeah?" asked an old man taking a walk who was presumably also named Gabe.

Justin felt bad for not sparing a few minutes to talk to him since the old man looked kind of lonely, but he had a mission. He sped down the sidewalk, ignoring the stitch in his side and the lack of oxygen in his lungs.

"Gabe!" he squeaked.

He could hear Spork running right behind him. He wished Spork were falling behind so that Justin had an excuse to slow down, but the younger kid seemed to be doing just fine.

Justin could no longer say, "Gabe!" anymore. He could dub it into the video or add subtitles later.

Oh, he was feeling the pain. He should've worn better shoes. This was dumb. He wasn't a runner. He was going into a career where you paid other people to run for you.

They wouldn't want to include the unedited video of him running anyway, so he could stop now. After all, he'd gone almost two blocks already. When they got closer to Gabe's house, he'd run the last fifty or sixty feet, and they'd edit it together so that it looked like one continuous sprint.

He glanced back over his shoulder to tell Spork the plan. Or at least make random gasping sounds that Spork would hopefully translate as the plan.

If this were a movie, this was the part where a car would come out of nowhere and smack into him. The "vehicle coming out of nowhere" trick had been used in countless movies, and even though it happened in a split second, you could always kind of tell that it was about to occur. From *Final Destination* to *Mean Girls* to *The Devil's Rejects* to *Whiplash* to *Fat Kid Rules the World* to the *Dawn of the Dead* remake to *Meet Joe Black* to *Bride of Chucky* to *Dreamcatcher* to *Constantine* to *Identity* and on and on and on, the trick of a vehicle flattening a character without warning was a common one.

And technically, since Spork was following him with a camera, this *was* a movie.

The car—a small one but still a car—smacked into him, and everything cut to black.

21

WHEN JUSTIN OPENED HIS EYES, HE WONDERED IF
this was a dream sequence.

Since he was floating above a lion pit in his underwear while
turnips with monocles played xylophones, he decided that he
probably was.

When Justin opened his eyes for real, he was lying in a hospital
bed. His body hurt all over. Mom and Dad were sitting next to
him, looking concerned, which was much better than them looking like, "Boy, do we have a dumb kid."

"What happened?" Justin asked.

"You got hit by a car," Mom told him.

"Am I okay?"

"You broke your arm."

"Off?"

"No. Just a fracture. Tons of bruises. Probably a mild concussion. It could have been a lot worse. You could have died."

"So no splatter?"

"No splatter."

"Oh, thank goodness. Is the driver okay?"

"She said that you just ran in front of her driveway while she was backing out without looking where you were going."

"That doesn't sound like something I'd do."

"It's in the video. The one made by that kid, Snork."

"Spork. Don't be disrespectful."

"It shows you running down the sidewalk shouting like a crazy person," said Dad. "I feel like maybe filmmaking and your brain don't mix well."

"I was playing to the camera for entertainment value," said Justin. "I'm not going to pretend that it's the smartest thing I've ever done because it's clearly not."

Justin looked around. He could get a lot of good production value out of this hospital if somebody brought him a camera, though he didn't think this was the best time to make such a request.

"We could have lost you forever," said Mom, wiping away a tear.

Justin started to make a joke about how he would have come back as a zombie, but again, poor timing.

The doctor, a middle-aged man with a neatly trimmed gray mustache and goatee, walked into the room. "How are you feeling, Justin?" he asked.

"I'm in a lot of pain."

"Of course you are. They make medicine to help with that, but then how would you learn your lesson? Let's talk about your arm. You're a fan of zombie movies, right?"

"Yes."

"During the zombie apocalypse, if you broke your arm like this, you'd be dead. Zombie apocalypse survival tip #127 says, 'Try not to break your arm.' If a zombie is coming at you with its mouth wide open, a broken arm is just going to flop around, and you'll drop your gun. That's a helpful little tidbit you can share with your friends." The doctor gave him a friendly grin.

"Uh, thanks?"

"You can thank me by not running in front of any more moving vehicles. Zombie apocalypse survival tip #398 says, 'Don't run in front of cars.' That's sound advice even when there's not a zombie apocalypse happening. What I'm saying, Justin, is that there are smart things we do in life, and then there are things we do that aren't so smart. They're all learning opportunities, but in particular we can learn from the ones that aren't that bright. I'm not actually going to poke at your arm because that would be unprofessional. But if I did, it would hurt even more than it does now, and it would help drive home my point that you should pay attention when you run."

"I will from now on. I promise."

"No need to promise me. Poor life choices are what keep me employed. But when paramedics bring in a dead kid, nobody enjoys that. It ruins everybody's day. So in summary, when you have the option to do something unintelligent, such as, say, running in front of a car, or the option to do something less unintelligent, such as, say, not running in front of a car, I hope that you'll think back to your current level of discomfort and make the right choice. Thank you for your attention."

The doctor left.

"I'm sorry I scared you," Justin told his parents. "It won't happen again."

Mom gave him a kiss on his forehead. "Your friends are also worried about you. They're in the waiting room. I'll send them in to say hi, and then you can get some sleep."

"Get some sleep…at home, right?"

"No, they want you to stay overnight for observation. Concussion, remember?"

Justin didn't remember. Maybe that was a sign of a concussion.

"I can't spend the night here," said Justin. "I'm supposed to be making a movie!"

"You have more important things to worry about right now, sweetheart."

"If I don't finish the movie, my mangled arm will be all for nothing!"

"It's not mangled."

"I have to finish what I started, or I'll regret it for the rest of my life. I'll be branded as the kid who didn't finish his movie. That's not the brand I want, Mom!"

"We'll discuss your movie later. But your behavior before the accident was enough to justify staying in the hospital for observation, so you're lucky it's only one night."

"All right. I understand. I won't try to escape."

"I never said anything about you trying to escape. Were you really thinking about trying to escape?"

"No, Mom."

"Anyway, I'll send your friends in, and then we'll be back to tuck you in."

Mom and Dad left. If he wanted to, Justin figured that he could sneak out of the hospital pretty easily. But if he did that, his parents would ground him for two years, and he didn't want that to happen until after the movie was done. He'd stay here tonight.

Spork hurried into the room. "Whoa! You got creamed by a car! Wham! I've never seen anything like that before!" Spork's expression grew very serious. "As soon as you got hit, I set down the camera and tried to help you. I'm sorry. I should have gotten more footage, but I wanted to make sure you weren't dead."

"It's okay."

After Spork left, Bobby came into the room. "How are you feeling?"

"Cracked."

"Well, we all miss you back on the movie set. It's just not the same without a director or producer or cameraman. It feels less like making a movie and more like just standing around and wondering what's going on."

"I'll be back tomorrow," Justin assured him.

"Did you hear about the lady whose car you hit with your body?"

"What about her?"

"She was in a horrible accident fifteen years ago. So awful that she's refused to leave the house since then. After in-home therapy three times a week for all this time, she'd finally worked up the courage to get behind the wheel of a car again."

"Did Uncle Clyde tell you to say that?"

Bobby grinned. "Yeah. I wish I had his wit."

"How's the lady really?"

"She's just mad. No mental trauma."

"Have you talked to Gabe?"

"Yeah."

"How is he?"

"I think he's getting tired of sitting in the waiting room."

"He's here?"

"Of course. He wouldn't refuse to visit you in the hospital. You fought over a movie, not a girl."

"Bring him in."

"I feel like you're moving past the subject of me pretty quickly. I know that getting beat up by a girl doesn't have the glamour of getting hit by a car, but still. Maybe you could ask me a question or two about how things are going first."

"Did Uncle Clyde tell you to say that?"

"No, it's just basic human decency. Duh."

"How are things going with you, Bobby?"

"Eh."

"Good to know."

"I'll go get Gabe."

For a split second—not even that long—Justin thought that Gabe was so distraught over what happened that he'd given himself a purple Mohawk, but no, it was Alicia. Justin wondered if the doctor was fibbing about not having given him pain medication.

"How's your arm?" she asked.

"It felt better when it wasn't broken. But it's my left arm, and I'm right-handed, so that's convenient. I've broken this arm before. No big deal."

"How's your head?"

"Not too bad. How's yours?"

Alicia had a large piece of gauze taped over her infected eyebrow. "A nurse patched it up. I've decided that not every face was meant to have jewelry in it. I'm going to let it heal, and then when I turn eighteen, I'm going to get a tattoo there."

"A solid plan."

"I guess you're not going to finish the movie, huh?"

"Why would you say that?"

"You've got an ouchie."

"One broken arm isn't going to stop me," said Justin. "Two broken arms? Maybe. One arm broken in six places? Probably. But one fracture in one arm? Not a chance."

"They said you also might have a concussion."

"Concussion, schmuncussion. I was acting like somebody whose head had smacked into the cement long before it actually happened. Tomorrow morning the movie is back on. Learn your lines."

"Whatever you say," said Alicia. She gave him a smile that made his heart soar and his arm stop hurting for a couple of seconds. Then she gave him a gentle kiss on his cast and left the room.

Christopher walked into the room before Justin could fully process what had just happened. "How're you feeling?"

"Why didn't you all come into the room together?" Justin asked.

"Only one minor is allowed in the room at a time. At least as of this afternoon. There was a toilet-papering incident on another floor. A man nearly lost his life."

"Got it. I'm feeling fine."

"Great. Even if this movie crashes and burns, I want you to know that it was a fantastic experience for me because I got to spend a lot of time with Alicia. You don't usually get to see the really hostile side of somebody before you're dating them, so this was refreshing. It should have scared me away, but weirdly enough, it made me like her even more. Isn't that funny?"

"I'm feeling kind of tired," said Justin. "I guess I should get some sleep. Could you send in Gabe?"

"Uncle Clyde is right outside."

"No, no, that's all right. I don't want to give him any germs from my broken arm."

Christopher left. Daisy walked into the room.

"I don't know you very well," she said, "so I have nothing to say, but it would be rude not to pay my respects."

"That's cool," said Justin. "Thanks."

"Talk to you later."

"Okay."

Daisy left. If Uncle Clyde stepped into the room, Justin was going to seriously consider flinging a piece of expensive hospital equipment at his head, but the next visitor was Gabe.

"Hi," said Gabe.

"Hi," said Justin.

"Hi," said Gabe again. "How'd the shoot go after I left?"

"Pretty decent. Got a lot of nice stuff with Alicia and Christopher. The zombies are going to be really cool. The car thing was kind of a bummer, but overall it was a productive day."

"Glad to hear it."

"I was on my way to ask you to come back to the movie."

"I know. I saw the video. It's very unsettling."

"I haven't seen it yet."

"You'll be happier if you skip it. I'm not trying to be mean, but it's almost a relief when the car hits you."

"I was trying to be entertaining."

"Sometime we'll brainstorm other ways to accomplish that."

"I was getting ready to shoot the first zombie scene, and I couldn't do it. I don't want to make this movie without you. If I was going to do that, I could've made it over the summer on a realistic schedule. I don't want realism. I want you to make this movie with me. Will you accept my apology?"

"Will it come with a change in behavior?"

"It might."

"The reasons I quit are still valid," said Gabe. "You've got a 'descending into madness' vibe going on, and I don't think it's working for you. If I come back to the project, it has to stop. It's fine to be passionate, just not scary passionate, okay?"

"That's acceptable."

"You said you wanted to make the greatest zombie movie ever. I tried to rein you in. But you got reined in too far because suddenly we weren't trying to make something that was great. We were trying to make something that was finished. That isn't what we set out to do. We need—"

"Hold on," said Justin. "How inspirational is this going to be?"

Gabe shrugged. "I don't know. Average, I guess."

"We need Spork in here getting it on video."

"Only one minor is allowed in the room at a time."

"Sure, if you follow the rules. But we're independent filmmakers, and we don't follow the rules. What's the hospital going to do, un-set my broken bone? We represent the spirit of guerrilla filmmaking, and we need to prove it to the world."

"Honestly I'm totally fine just saying the inspirational stuff to you."

"Well, I look like a fool in the behind-the-scenes footage, and it would be nice to get a chance to redeem myself."

"I'll go get him."

Gabe left the room and returned a moment later with Spork.

"I'm going to say that thing about independent filmmakers again," said Justin. He looked directly into the camera. "Sure, if you follow the rules. But we're—"

"Why would we have video of you talking about wanting to get video?" Gabe asked. "That doesn't make any sense."

"It doesn't need to make sense."

"We're backsliding already."

"No, we're not. We'll put 'Reenactment' up on the screen. Just let me do this."

"Okay. Proceed."

"Sure, if you follow the rules. But we're independent film-makers, and. We. Don't. Follow. The. Rules. Remember that, future generations who are watching this. We represent the spirit of guerrilla filmmaking. We *are* filmmaking."

Justin motioned for Spork to point the camera at Gabe.

"You said you wanted to make the greatest zombie movie ever. I tried to fence you in."

"Rein," Justin corrected.

"You're right. I tried to rein you in. But you got reined in too far because suddenly we weren't trying to make something that was great."

"A little slower…and more emotion. Make the viewer feel the power of your words."

"You're right. I tried—"

"Look at me, not the camera."

"You're right. I tried—"

"Still rushing a bit. Just close your eyes and take a deep breath. Relax your whole body. Raise your shoulders, tilt your head back, and just breathe in, breathe out. Very good."

"My battery is almost dead," said Spork.

"Thanks for the warning," said Justin. "Action!"

"But you got reined in too far because suddenly we weren't trying to make something that was great. We were trying to make something that was finished. That isn't what we set out to do. We need to return to the original inspiration, to *your* original inspira-tion, and we need to make the greatest zombie movie ever!"

"Yes!" Justin wanted to jump out of his bed and give Gabe a great big hug, but if he was only going to do smart things from now on, a good start would be to not jostle his broken bone.

"They all say we can't do it," said Gabe. "And yeah, our first day kind of proves them right. But you know what? Now we're going to prove them wrong!"

"Who says we can't do it?" Justin asked.

"Oh, it's all over social media. You might want to stay offline for a while."

"You know what? Let them laugh. It'll make us stronger."

"I still want to make this movie, but I can't have you acting all Captain Ahab from *Moby-Dick* the whole time. Ahab was not a well-adjusted man. This movie can't be your white whale."

"I understand."

"And yet at the same time, I need you to be *more* like Ahab because what you were doing right before I quit is like if he said, 'I must kill the white whale! I must kill the white whale! Actually no, I'll just kill a halibut instead.'"

"I'm not completely sure where you stand on this issue," said Justin. "A few days ago, you were in the cafeteria, sarcastically pretending to try to jump up and grab the sun."

"I want you to be like Ahab if his goal wasn't something ridiculous like to catch that one specific white whale out of all the whales in the ocean, but he still wanted to catch something awesome. Like maybe a great white shark. He chose a shark because he had access to the appropriate resources to catch one, and…I think I'm confusing myself on where I stand on the issue. Let's just make the greatest zombie movie ever, okay?"

"Okay."

WHEN JUSTIN WOKE UP, HE WAS AT HOME IN HIS
own bed.

He wondered if he was dreaming again, and then he noticed
the polka-dotted lobsters parachuting from the ceiling. So yep,
he was.

He woke up in the hospital bed.

A man was seated next to him.

Justin was fortunate enough to have lived the kind of sheltered
existence where he didn't spend a lot of time around mob enforcers.
However, if he were forced to guess this gentleman's career (possi-
bly at gunpoint by a mobster), mob enforcer would have been one
of his top three guesses. The other two guesses were much more
dangerous, so he hoped the man was indeed from the mob.

"Hello, Justin," said the man. He looked like he was about
fifty, and there was a deep scar under his right eye.

"Uh, hi?"

"I'm a quote unquote *friend* of your grandmother's."

Justin quickly sat up. "I see."

"Apparently she has a financial investment in a motion picture that you are currently in the process of making."

"Yes, sir."

"And apparently she's beginning to worry about the security of her investment. How secure is her investment, Justin?"

"It's secure. It's very secure."

The man looked at Justin as if gazing into his soul. "I hope you're telling me the truth. I'd hate to have you meet up with another quote unquote *accident*."

"Another one?"

"Do you really think that your getting hit by a car was a coincidence?"

Justin gaped at him. "You mean it wasn't a…" He stopped gaping. "Yes, it was. Nobody could have predicted that I'd be running down the sidewalk like that."

"Good work, Justin. You've found the hole in my story. I am not responsible for your broken arm. But that does not mean your arm is safe from me, if you know what I mean."

"She'll get her twelve percent return on her investment. I promise."

"Then you have nothing to fear from me."

"Thank you."

The man started to rise from his seat but then sat back down and sighed. "I can't believe she's got me going after teenagers. That's not where I wanted to be at this point in my career. I thought I'd be intimidating politicians or wealthy businessmen, not protecting some kid's grandmother's five thousand bucks. This is ridiculous. How much do you think she's paying me? Go on, guess."

"I have no idea."

"Guess."

"Three thousand dollars?"

"She's paying me nothing. She's paying me in *experience* like I'm some kind of intern. Can you believe that?"

"Well, you don't *have* to do it, do you?"

"If only that were true. Your grandma is vicious, Justin. I hate to be the one to break that news to you, but she is. I don't know if she was born that way or if the circumstances of her life made her that way, but the woman is a monster."

"Jeez," said Justin.

"I'm not saying that she's the devil. And I'm not playing that trick where I say that she's not the devil and you relax, and then I say that she's *worse* than the devil. She's not as bad as the devil. But she's awful and frightening, and I very strongly recommend that you finish this movie and earn back her money."

"I will."

"Good. You don't want to see me here again."

"I definitely don't."

"Or someplace else. I don't only show up in hospital rooms after dark. There's no place that you're safe from me. I'm not trying to traumatize you. Just being honest."

"I appreciate your honesty."

The man stood up. "Anyway, I'm gonna get out of here and try to get some sleep. Remember what I said. I think we had a pleasant conversation, even if I did most of the talking, but next time it'll be less of a conversation and more along the lines of you screaming a lot. Got it?"

"Got it."

"Do you remember if I take a left or a right at the end of this hallway? I'm not great with directions."

"I'm not sure. I woke up here."

"Okay. It was inappropriate of me to ask in the first place. I'll figure it out. See ya later."

"Unless I finish the movie and make back Grandma's investment, right?"

"Right, right. I was just being polite. 'See ya later' wasn't meant to imply that I was going to renege on our agreement. Get some sleep, kid."

Justin slept poorly.

He was released in the morning. As the nurse wheeled him down the hallway, Justin decided not to tell his parents about his encounter in the middle of the night. Maybe it was a dream, or maybe it was indeed a trainee mobster there to deliver a stern warning. Either way, it was best not to worry them.

Justin was going to miss the hospital gown. It was the most comfortable thing he'd ever worn. When he was a massively successful director and owned his own island, hospital gowns would be the mandatory dress code.

As he sat in the backseat of the car, he tried to figure out the best way to ask them to drop him off at Uncle Clyde's house so we could get back to work. There probably wasn't a perfect way to ask this. Still, if he was clever, he could phrase it in such a way that they didn't immediately scream, "Are you out of your mind?"

"Before you ask, you're not going anywhere today," said Mom, glancing back at him.

"You already knew that, right?" asked Dad, glancing up at

Justin's reflection in the rearview mirror since he was the one driving. "I mean, it's only common sense."

"I knew that you might lean in that direction," said Justin. "But it's truly not necessary. My arm actually feels better than it did before I broke it. Maybe it had too much marrow before."

"You need to rest for at least a day."

"Nah, I'm the director. My job is to order people around. As long as I don't break my jaw, I'm fine."

"This isn't open for discussion," said Dad.

"I completely understand. You want to keep me safe, and it's not only for emotional reasons. There are also legal factors involved. But really, people break their arms every day. Literally every single day, arms go crunch, crunch, crunch. It's not a big deal. I'm not going to do anything silly like lift weights or dangle from a tree branch or exercise."

"You're working under the impression that you're going to be able to change our minds," said Mom. "You're not."

They really didn't sound like they were going to budge on this issue. What other tactics could he use? Temper tantrum? It had been a few years since he'd gone that route, but…

"And if you try to sneak out, you'll be grounded basically forever," said Dad.

"If I tried to sneak out, it would mean that I was climbing out a second-story window, which is exactly the kind of thing I'm promising not to do. I swear I won't get hurt again. I'll be like some prima donna celebrity and make a rule that nobody can get within fifty feet of me. C'mon, please. I can't afford to lose a whole day."

"Sorry," said Mom, not sounding sorry.

"This is really important to me."

"We get that. And it's why you only have to stay home for one day. But that one day is not negotiable."

What was Justin going to do? Maybe there was a way he could turn his parents against each other. What was their last argument about? Dad had left the butter on the kitchen counter, right?

No, creating strife in their marriage would be wrong. He'd have to resign himself to his accursed fate.

In theory, he could ask Gabe and Bobby to carry on without him for one day. But his rule that he didn't want to make the movie without Gabe had darn well *better* work both ways. If they tried to make the movie without him, he'd have the most legendary meltdown in the history of humankind. He wouldn't even pretend that he was okay with it. He'd just start destroying things. He wouldn't even *faux*-suggest it with the expectation that they'd say no, because if they hesitated for even the tiniest fraction of a second before the word no came out of their mouths, he'd totally lose it. Justin understood this about himself, and he was okay with it.

"Can Gabe and Bobby at least come over?" Justin asked.

"No," said Dad.

"*No?*" Justin asked, having expected a different answer.

"No," said Mom.

"Why not? Do you think they're going to bounce a basketball off my concussion?"

"Because what you need," said Dad, "is some rest. You're not going to get any rest if you're upstairs freaking out about your movie. Cinema will still exist on Monday."

"You're becoming villains in my life story. You realize this, right?"

"Someday you'll think back on this with a brain that isn't permanently damaged because of our excellent parental care and thank us," said Dad.

Justin scowled at him. He was too mature to pout, but he decided to sulk for the rest of the ride home. Then he decided that sulking was also beneath him, and he went for a mild, simmering rage. He knew that they were doing this for his own good. He didn't care. His own good was overrated. He'd worry about his own good when the movie was finished.

If he lost all of today, his chances of finishing the movie were essentially nonexistent, right? Now that making a good movie was important again, the lack of time was even more problematic.

He texted Gabe and asked him to spread the message that today's shoot was canceled.

I figured, Gabe texted back.

We'll make up the time, Justin texted. This movie is going to get cone.

Cone?

Done. Stupid autocorrect.

Why would autocorrect change done to cone?

Fine. I typed cone by mistake. Are u happy?

The lies need to stop, Justin. The lies need to stop.

You probably think we'll never finish now.

We'll figure something out.

When Justin got home, he took a couple of aspirin and went up to his room. He'd been focusing on his frustration about *Dead Skull*, but he also had to admit that having a broken arm wasn't exactly pleasant. It was starting to itch like crazy, and since he wasn't permitted to crack open his cast and go after the itch with a fork, he just had to sit there and try not to think about how much it itched, which was impossible because of how much it itched, itched, itched.

He lay down on his bed and stared at the ceiling. There was nothing interesting up there.

He'd take a quick nap and then sort things out.

When he woke up, it was time for dinner.

He ate dinner and went back to sleep.

2 3

THE NEXT DAY AT SCHOOL WAS GREAT, OR TO BE

more specific, not great.

"How's the movie going?" the other kids asked him in a tone that made it pretty clear that they knew exactly how the movie was going. They just wanted to chuckle when he answered, "It's going fine."

"How'd you break your arm?" kids also asked him. They knew how he broke his arm. Everybody knew how he broke his arm. And they all knew about the element of stupidity involved. They had to. They were all grinning when they asked it, and Kid Breaks Arm after Getting Hit by Car was tragic out of context.

At lunchtime Justin, Gabe, and Bobby sat in the cafeteria, all of them frowning.

"I wish the story about Alicia beating me up hadn't circulated so quickly," said Bobby. "I knew it would get out to the public, but I was expecting maybe sixty or sixty-five percent audience awareness. I think we're at ninety-eight percent. That kid who doesn't speak English didn't know, but somebody mimed it for him."

"What's worse is that you did your job as a sound guy poorly," said Gabe.

"No, that's not worse at all. Do you know what people are calling me?"

"What?"

"Guy Who Got Beat Up by Alicia Howtz."

"That's seriously your new nickname?" asked Justin. "That's the best they could do?"

"Yep."

"A whole school full of kids, and they can't come up with something inventive? That's not even a real nickname. That's just a description."

"I know. All day it was, 'Hey there, Guy Who Got Beat Up by Alicia Howtz.' I thought they might sarcastically call me Muscles or something like that, but nope."

"On the bright side," said Gabe, "it's not something people will be calling you twenty years from now. It's too inconvenient to say."

"Do you know what's weird?" Justin asked.

"Horses in princess costumes?" suggested Bobby.

Justin ignored him. "What's weird is that I don't regret this. I mean, I regret a lot of the individual decisions I made, and I regret the way most of it has turned out so far. But there's never been a point where I wished that I'd never decided to make this movie."

"I feel the same way," said Gabe.

"I feel a bit differently," said Bobby, "but overall, there were way more moments where I was happy that we were making this movie than there were sad moments that Alicia was hitting me with my own boom mic."

Gabe raised his container of chocolate milk in a toast. "No matter how it turns out, I'm glad we're doing this."

Justin and Bobby raised their own chocolate milks and tapped them together.

Zack Peterson, who used to fling volleyballs at Justin in second grade, walked by and sneered. "Hey, Guy Who Got Beat Up by Alicia Howtz, did your boyfriend break his arm trying to protect you?"

Bobby flung his chocolate milk at Zack and hit the center of his shirt. It doused him like a water balloon.

"You little geek!" Zack raised his fist and stepped forward.

"I fought the worst. Do you really think I'm scared of you?"

"Yeah, I guess that's a good point." Zack lowered his fist and continued on his way.

"Anyway," said Justin, "we're going to still try to cram everything into the rest of the shooting schedule. It turns out I can borrow a camera from the media center. I didn't tell them that I broke the old one, so please don't mention that in casual conversation. Saturday and Sunday are going to be all zombies all the time. We're going to get our biggest, most epic shots. Starting with our easiest stuff made it feel like we weren't accomplishing as much."

"So since we failed at the easy stuff, we're going to switch to the hard stuff?"

"Exactly. Go big or go home, right? Isn't that what people say on reality shows?"

"Constantly."

"And that's what we're going to do."

As Justin sat in his room, studying for his history test, his phone rang. It was Bobby.

"Hello?"

"Hi, Justin. Hey, you know how I usually like to have good news when I call?"

"Do you have good news?"

"Not really."

"What's wrong?"

"Maybe you should see it for yourself."

Justin and Bobby stood outside Uncle Clyde's house. They kept out of the way of the firemen as they watched the place burn.

"I wasn't smoking in bed!" Uncle Clyde insisted. "I was vaping! That's supposed to be one of the advantages to e-cigarettes. They don't burn your house down!"

The house was a complete inferno, including, presumably, the forty-nine hundred dollars' worth of zombie effects.

Justin felt like he was being a bit insensitive by recording all of this, but since he'd just lost the entirety of their amazing zombie army, he could live with his lack of empathy. They could easily add a new scene to the script where a house burned to the ground.

"It was insured, right?" Bobby asked his uncle.

Uncle Clyde shook his head. "I was in prison for insurance fraud, so no."

"I'll be back," said Justin. "I'm going to get a wide shot of the fire engines." Keeping focused on his work was the only way he could resist the urge to drop to his knees and scream, "Why? Why? *Why?*"

He got a bunch of shots from various angles, but he was busy filming the Dalmatian when the house collapsed, which gave him another reason to want to scream in frustration.

"There's one positive thing about this," said Bobby.

"What?"

"Nobody got hurt."

"Oh," said Justin. "I thought you meant a positive thing for us."

"They're keeping the fire contained, so none of his neighbors will have any damage to their property. Uncle Clyde didn't own any pets, so no animals were harmed, and no humans had to put themselves in danger to rescue the pets."

"I'm glad nobody was hurt. It means that we can focus on our own loss without being selfish and horrible people."

"I think we can salvage this," said Bobby. "What do you think of this new title? *Night of the Melted Dead.*"

"Are you kidding?" asked Justin.

"You don't see melted zombies very often."

"Even if that was a good idea—and I'd like to emphasize that it's a bad idea—the entire house collapsed into the basement. We can't rescue what's left of the burnt-up blobs of the prosthetics. We have no zombies."

"Maybe…maybe the twist is that it's a zombie movie, but we don't have any zombies. Like they're zombies of the mind."

"No," said Justin. "Hey, Uncle Clyde?"

Uncle Clyde took his electronic cigarette out of his mouth. "What do you want?"

"I still need zombies from you this weekend."

"I lost everything, kid. My furniture, my carpet, my collection of Kleenex used by famous people. I've got nothing. What am I supposed to do?"

"I'll get you the money to buy more supplies."

"How?"

"Let me worry about that."

"Plus labor?"

"No, you'll work for cookies."

Uncle Clyde shrugged. "If you can raise the money, I'll make your zombies."

"Did you really have a collection of Kleenex used by famous people?" asked Bobby.

"Yes. Well, no. They were people I hoped would become famous someday. None of them are yet." Uncle Clyde motioned to the ashes that were whirling in the air. "Their germs are all around us now. Who knows where they'll end up?"

"How are you going to get the money?" Bobby asked Justin.

"I'm going to use an untapped resource," said Justin. "My possessions."

Justin would miss his video game system and his awesome assortment of games to play on it deeply, but there were more important things in life.

He would miss his vast collection of movies even more. Oh, what wonderful times they'd shared. He treasured his memories of even the terrible ones, and losing all of these discs was going to hurt his heart. Still, he had his own movie to make.

All of his cool horror villain figures were also going to have to go. He'd been amassing this collection since he was nine, and a couple of the figures were impossible to find anymore. But this was something he needed to do. Maybe someday figures would be made from the characters of *his* movie.

Doofy, the stuffed bear he had gotten for his second birthday, was not going anywhere. Forget that. Production of Doofys had been discontinued when their noses were found to be a safety hazard to young children, and they fetched a lot of money in online auctions, but…no way. Doofy stayed.

Justin hated to sell all of his stuff, but he was too young for a credit card. He had three more years before he could get into crippling debt on his own.

He'd placed the ads and gotten back quick responses. He wouldn't come anywhere close to making five thousand dollars, but it would be *something*.

The doorbell rang. When he went downstairs and answered it, Gabe and Bobby were standing on his front porch. Each of them was holding a cardboard box.

"What's that?" Justin asked.

"*Star Wars* figures," said Bobby. "Unopened."

"Aren't those your dad's?"

"Yes. Someday I will suffer for this. Let's make it worth it."

"I've got *Simpsons* figures," said Gabe, "and a bunch of comic books."

"You guys don't have to do this," said Justin.

"Yes, we do," said Gabe. "We're in this together. Maybe we're spiraling into disaster, but if so, we're spiraling into disaster as a team."

"Thank you," said Justin. "This means everything to me."

They all stood there for a moment, waiting for one of them to make a stupid comment that would diminish the emotion of the moment, but nobody did.

2 4

ON SATURDAY MORNING JUSTIN AWOKE, GOT OUT
of bed, and did all of the things in his morning routine that now
took twice as long since he had a broken arm. At least he no
longer felt any pressure to do push-ups.

He loaded up his red wagon and headed off. The original plan
was to film the first set of epic zombie scenes on his own street,
but now that Uncle Clyde's home no longer existed, it provided a
better backdrop for a postapocalyptic landscape.

He met up with Gabe and Bobby, and they walked there
together. Uncle Clyde got out of his car, where he now lived, and
waved to them.

"What time do the zombies start showing up?" Uncle Clyde asked.

"Six."

"What time is it now? My watch stopped working after it
melted in the fire."

"Five till."

"Wake me when the first one gets here." Uncle Clyde got back
into his car and shut the door.

"Let's get some establishing shots of the street," said Justin.
"I'd kind of expected some of our zombies to be here early."

Bobby shrugged. "Zombies are prompt."

By the time they got their shots, it was a few minutes after six.

"Everybody knows it's 6:00 a.m., not p.m., right?" asked Gabe.

"Yes. I put 6:00 a.m., and then I put 'That means six in the morning,' in parentheses."

"Then where are they?"

"I don't know! I put flyers everywhere! I put fifty of them just in school, and I put them up all over town! I posted stuff all over the Internet, and I even placed an ad in the newspaper so we could get some old zombies. Last night I followed up with dozens of people who said they'd do it. Where is everybody?"

"I guess they'd rather sleep in."

"What kind of garbage is that? Who in their right mind would rather sleep than be a zombie in a movie? This should be everybody's *dream*! We're offering them this incredible opportunity, and they can't be bothered to show up?"

"Are you sure they have the right address?"

Justin reached into his pocket and took out a crumpled flier. He straightened it out, which was not easy with one hand, and held it up. "See? Everything's accurate."

"Yep. That's disappointing. I hoped it was our own incompetence and not a lack of interest."

"What are we going to do?" asked Bobby.

"We're going to get our zombies."

"Good morning, sir. I understand that it's very early, and I apologize for awakening you from your slumber. My name is Justin

Hollow, and I'm the director of the upcoming feature film *Dead Skull*. The title may change, but we're filming in your neighborhood today. I was wondering if you and your family would be interested in gaining your own piece of cinematic immortality by playing zombies?"

"Go away," the man said before he shut the door in Justin's face.

"I know that you're trying to sound professional," Gabe told Justin, "but when I hear 'awaken from slumber,' I think about ancient evils awakening after a hundred years."

"Noted."

"Good morning, ma'am. I would apologize for waking you up so early, but obviously I *didn't* wake you up because nobody looks that good right out of bed. Anyway—"

The woman slammed the door in his face.

"Compliments before 7:00 a.m. are creepy," said Gabe.

"I wasn't hitting on her! I was trying to be nice!"

"Be less nice next time."

"Noted."

"Good morning, sir. I apologize for bothering you so early. My name is Justin Hollow, and I'm the director of the upcoming feature film *Dead Skull*."

"You recruiting for a cult?"

"No, sir. No cult here. We're just making a movie."

"A recruitment film for a cult?"

"No, there's nothing cultish about what we're doing. It's a zombie movie."

"Do you mean like zombies who shave their heads and do everything the cult leader says?"

"No, no, I assure you that's not it at all. I mean, our lead actress did shave most of her head, but it wasn't a cult sort of thing. These zombies are reanimated corpses that feast upon the flesh of the living."

"That's fine. As long as it's not a cult."

"No, sir. Not a cult."

"My sister joined a cult in college. They wouldn't let her eat vegetables or write with her left hand. Everybody had to wear tinted glasses, even on cloudy days. And every other Wednesday they sacrificed a goat to the Dark One."

"That's pretty far from what this is. Do you want to be a zombie in our movie?"

"Nah, but I wish you luck."

"Good morning, ma'am."

"Do you know what time it is?"

"Yes, and I apologize."

"What in the *world* do you want?"

"My name is Herman Flipperson," said Justin, deciding on the spot that giving the woman his real name was not a good idea. "I'm director of the upcoming feature film... You know, I'm seeing a lot of rage in your eyes, and I think my partners and I have decided to quietly back away and leave you alone."

The woman shut the door in his face.

"Has humanity really become so antisocial that you can't even go door-to-door anymore without people getting mad at you?" Justin asked.

"She's peeking through the window," said Bobby. "And I saw a shotgun hanging on her wall."

"Okay, let's get out of here. But we'll record the house from someplace safe in case she does open fire."

"Good morning, ma'am. I see that your scary dog really doesn't want us here, so we'll move along. Thank you for your time."

"Good morning. Is your mommy or daddy home?"

"Gah?"

"Your mommy? Your daddy?"

"Gah?"

"Do you like zombies? Zombies?" Justin held out his arms and made a face like a zombie.

The three-year-old began to cry.

"Run! Run!" said Justin, fleeing from the scene.

"Good morning, sir. My name is Justin Hollow, noted film director. My films include *Mummy Pit*, *Werewolf Night*, and *Ghost Barn*. Sadly I've met with an unfortunate accident that has cost me the use of my left arm. Pain shoots through it with every breath I take. But I'm not here for sympathy, and I'm not letting that stop me from making my first feature-length motion picture. That's where *you* come in! The hour is early, but it's never too early to play a zombie! I'm here to offer you and your loved ones the opportunity to portray a member of the living dead in a film that's sure to get the critics raving!"

The man narrowed his eyes. "Do I have to pay for this?"

"Oh, goodness no, sir. And the best part is that you can keep all of the latex we stick to your face, absolutely free!"

"Yeah, all right. I'll go put on some pants."

"Good morning, sir and ma'am. You're a lovely couple. My name is Bobby. My partner here, Justin, is making a movie. As you can see, he suffered a horrific on-set injury, so I'm doing the talking to ease his burden. Are you feeling okay, Justin?"

Justin nodded and coughed gently.

"Justin has but one dream—to make a movie. And he's trying to fulfill that dream right now with the time he has left. To make that dream come true, he's not asking for money—"

"Though he would not decline it," said Gabe.

"What he needs are zombies. Lots of zombies. This is your chance to make a young boy's final wish come true."

"So you're making a zombie movie?"

"With your help, we are."

"Like *28 Days Later*?"

"Yes, sir."

"Well, they aren't zombies in *28 Days Later*. They're the infected. You don't know what you're talking about."

The man shut the door in their faces.

Bobby rang the doorbell. The man opened the door again.

"We're aware of the difference between the infected and true members of the living dead," said Justin. "We just felt that it would be inappropriate to correct you when we're asking for a favor. I completely understand where you're coming from. But like it or not, our culture has decided that *28 Days Later* is a legitimate zombie movie, and to get worked up about it is a bit pedantic."

"So are you calling me pedantic because I care about the true definitions of zombies? If I don't care, who will?"

"I didn't say full-on pedantic. Just a bit pedantic."

"Are you doing fast zombies or slow zombies?"

"Both."

"*What?* That's not how it works!"

"You haven't even read the script. You're prejudging something before you know anything about it. It's like we knocked on the door of the Internet."

"Look, there are advantages and disadvantages to both, but there is no realistic world in which slow zombies and fast zombies would coexist. You have to choose your side. When you watch the Super Bowl, you don't get to root for both teams. You pick one, and you hope that the other one gets *destroyed*."

"The fact that you're so passionate about this leads me to believe that you're a slow zombie guy," said Gabe.

"Darn right."

Gabe high-fived the man.

"We won't have any fast zombies in your scene if you agree to be in our movie," said Justin.

"Yeah, okay. Let me wake up the kids."

"Good morning. Oh, hi, Alicia."

"Hi." Alicia stood there in a nightgown, looking confused. "Did I miss my call time?"

"No, no, we're just doing some zombie recruitment. I didn't know you lived here."

"Yeah. It's kind of early to be going door-to-door, don't you think?"

"That's what the people in this neighborhood keep telling me. Your eyebrow looks a lot better."

"Thanks. It finally stopped leaking a couple of days ago."

"That's going to be a continuity issue," said Gabe.

"Knock it off," Justin told him. "What do you want her to do, infect it again on purpose?"

Justin loved that a girl of her stunning beauty was willing to answer the front door in an ugly tan nightgown. He loved that she was willing to discuss the grosser aspects of her eyebrow. In fact, now that the shock had worn off, he liked the feisty manner in which she'd overreacted to Bobby dropping the boom mic.

He feared rejection, but he'd been rejected by about fifty-three people this morning. And if he was going to make a movie without a safety net, why not start living his life that way too?

"Alicia, do you want to go to Monkey Burger with me sometime?"

"You mean to discuss the movie?"

Justin shook his head. "I mean as a date."

"Oh." Alicia suddenly looked uncomfortable. "I can't date my director. I'm sorry. That wouldn't be professional. You understand, right?"

"Yes, yes, yes, yes, yes, I completely understand. Yes." *Don't bail on this*, Justin told himself. *Don't wuss out, even though Gabe and Bobby are right here to witness the brutal sting of eternal humiliation.* "What about after the movie is done?"

"You'll always have been my director," said Alicia. "So I don't think it would work."

"That makes sense. Sorry for waking you up."

"You didn't wake me up. I was watching *King Kong*."

King Kong! Oh, how he loved her!

Justin felt like he'd been kicked in the face by Mr. Kong, but he tried not to let it show. "Well, I'll see you on the set. Gotta go round up more zombies."

"Good luck."

Justin, Gabe, and Bobby left.

"Dude, that was harsh," said Gabe.

"It wasn't harsh. She could have spat at me…or squirted her eyebrow at me."

"I mean that Bobby and I were there to witness it."

"Doesn't bother me at all," said Justin as King Kong continued stomping on his head. "Let's go get the rest of our zombies."

25

WHEN THEY RETURNED TO THE SET, UNCLE CLYDE
was hurriedly applying zombie makeup to the newly recruited
cast. They had eight zombies, which was 492 fewer than Justin
wanted. But the two that were done were very cool zombies, and
quality was more important than quantity—at least that was
what he told himself. Spork was walking around, taking video
and interviewing the zombies about their motivation.

"Which one is the eyeball-munching zombie?" Justin asked Uncle
Clyde. "I want to get that shot while you make up the rest of them."

"You didn't tell me you wanted the eyeball-munching
zombie first."

"Yes, I did. I taped a note to your windshield." Justin pointed
to a note taped to Uncle Clyde's windshield that read, *We need the
eyeball-munching zombie first.*

"Oh. I thought it was a citation. Ummm…" Uncle Clyde
looked around at the available actors. "None of these will work.
I'll have to use Bobby."

"Who?" asked Bobby.

"Sit down on the makeup chair, Bobby," said Uncle Clyde,
gesturing to the front hood of his car.

"Oh, no. I don't like having things glued to my face."

"Sit down, Bobby."

"I can't. I have to record sound."

"I don't think we can get usable sound anyway, unless that guy finishes mowing his lawn," said Justin. "This will be your cameo."

"My cameo was supposed to be the guy in yoga pants."

"You can still play him. You won't be recognizable as a zombie."

"Are you going to pour blood on me?"

"A few drops."

"I wrote this scene, Justin. I know how much blood there is."

"A few pints then. Are you scared of a few pints of fake blood? It tastes fine. I had some on my cereal this morning."

"Why not have Gabe play him?"

"Because Gabe is our cameraman. And like it or not, every group has a dynamic, and in our group you've fallen into the role of designated abuse taker. Now sit down and get zombified."

Bobby sat down on the front hood. Uncle Clyde gestured to a wide variety of prosthetic wounds he'd created. "Which do you prefer?" Uncle Clyde asked. "Hole in chin? Bottom half of nose gone? Part of cheek hanging down like flap? Nail in face? Forehead burnt off? Chicken pox scars? Eyeball falling out?"

"It's probably too much to have his eyeball falling out when he's about to eat somebody's eyeball," said Justin.

"I disagree," said Uncle Clyde.

"Let's go with bottom half of nose gone."

"Can't I be somebody who just turned?" asked Bobby. "Not every zombie has to be unsightly."

"Make him really rotted," Justin told Uncle Clyde. "If I can eat a sandwich while I'm looking at him, I'm sending him back."

"Aye-aye, Cap'n."

Justin and Gabe set up the scene while Uncle Clyde went to work turning Bobby into a flesh-eater. Right on time, a very fancy car pulled up, and the actor playing Bobby's victim got out.

"Mr. Pamm!" said Justin to his boss. "Thanks for doing this for me!"

Mr. Pamm looked suspiciously at the actors. "Is this a monster movie?"

"Did I not tell you that?"

"No."

"Oh. My mistake. Thank you for wearing such a nice suit."

"I thought I was playing a romantic lead."

"You are. It's just not a traditional romantic lead. In your character's backstory, he's a handsome, charming, dapper man who's beloved by his entire community."

"That sounds okay."

"Now when we meet him in this movie, he's getting his eyeball eaten by a zombie, but I don't want you to think about that. I want you to think about how handsome you *used* to look."

"Did you mislead me about this role?"

"That doesn't sound like something I would do. Uncle Clyde, are you ready to take out Mr. Pamm's eye?"

"Action!"

Mr. Pamm lay on his back on the street, thrashing around in terror as Zombie Bobby sat on top on him, snarling.

"Eat the eyeball!" shouted Justin. "Eat it!"

Bobby leaned down and bit down on Mr. Pamm's phony dangling eyeball.

"I can't do it!" Bobby said. "It tastes just like a real one!"

"Eat it!"

Bobby chomped down on the eyeball. "It burst in my mouth!"

"Stop talking! Our zombies don't talk!"

Mr. Pamm screamed. "My eye! My dang eye!"

"Get ready with the blood!" Justin called to the zombie extras who'd been promoted to blood pourers. "Bobby, pretend that you're enjoying the eyeball!"

Bobby chewed the eyeball, looking like he was trying not to gag.

"Don't swallow it," said Justin. "It's not edible. Blood in three…two…one. *Dump it!*"

The extras poured three buckets of blood onto Bobby and Mr. Pamm.

"More blood!" Justin shouted. "Way more blood!"

The extras each picked up their second buckets of blood.

"Shouldn't we be saving some of that blood for later?" asked Gabe.

"We'll make more. More blood in three…two…"

"Dang it, get off me, you dang zombie!" shouted Mr. Pamm. He spat out some of the syrup with red food coloring in it. "My eye! I can only see half as well without that eye!"

"One! Dump the blood! Dump the blood!"

Three more buckets of blood splashed over Bobby and Mr. Pamm.

"You said it was only going to be three buckets!" Bobby wailed.

"Stop talking! Everybody get ready for the next blood round. Gabe, get a shot of it pouring down into the gutter."

"Already done."

The zombie extras each picked up another bucket.

"Who is this blood supposed to be coming out of?" asked Gabe.

"It doesn't matter. Three…two…one. *Drench them!*"

Three more buckets of blood came down upon Bobby and Mr. Pamm.

"Cue the intestines!" said Justin.

"I don't want to eat any intestines!" said Bobby. "Please!"

"Three…two…one. *Yank them!*"

Bobby dug his fingers into the fake stomach that Uncle Clyde had glued to Mr. Pamm. He grabbed a handful of intestine and began to pull it out.

"Keep pulling!"

"It's too slippery! I can't hold it!"

"Keep pulling!"

"My intestines! My dang intestines!"

"More blood!"

More blood rained down upon the ferocious zombie and his victim.

"Gnaw on it! Gnaw, Bobby! Gnaw!"

"I don't want to gnaw!"

"Do it for America!"

Bobby shoved a segment of the intestines into his mouth and bit down.

"Pretend you like it! To you it's delicious!"

"It's horrible!"

"It's fake! It's just rubber!"

"Well, actually…" said Uncle Clyde.

"We're almost done!" said Justin. "One last slurp!"

"I'm dead!" said Mr. Pamm. "I'm dang dead!"

"Cut!" said Justin. "Let's get them cleaned up for a second take."

"He's just kidding," said Gabe.

Bobby and Mr. Pamm stood up. "That was a lot of fun," said Mr. Pamm, grinning. "Thank you for inviting me."

"Anytime."

"Uh-oh," said Gabe, pointing to the approaching vehicle. "Looks like somebody called the cops."

"What were we doing that would make somebody call the police?" Justin asked. "Get as many angles of the car as you can. Don't stop unless they whack you with a nightstick."

"Will do."

The car parked behind Uncle Clyde's car, and two stern-looking officers got out. Justin considered immediately telling them that it was not real blood covering the two people they were staring at, but he decided to let Gabe capture their reactions on video first.

"You kids making a movie?" asked the first officer.

"Yes, sir," said Justin, walking over to him.

"We've had a noise complaint."

"Right. Sorry. We were filming a scene where my boss got torn apart by a zombie, and we felt he would make some noise under those circumstances."

The officer looked Justin directly in the eye. "Do you know what I hate?"

"What?"

"I hate whiny neighbors." He reached down and picked up the intestines. "This is neat stuff. I loved to make movies when I was a kid. My brother and I made an alien invasion movie. You like aliens?"

"I sure do."

"You should make an alien movie someday. Anyway, I'm going to have to ask you to try to keep the volume down a bit.

Maybe just add the screams in postproduction. You're not going to leave all of the blood and guts on the street, right?"

"Absolutely not. Bobby will be cleaning all of that up as soon as we're done."

The second officer gestured to the mess. "I do have to say that in my twenty-two years on the force, I've seen some grisly things. I hate to criticize all of your hard work, but unfortunately you got the details of this type of attack wrong. It's not possible for this much blood to come out of a single human being."

"Why are you nitpicking?" asked the first officer, still holding the intestines.

"You weren't thinking the same thing?"

"No, it's stylized. They're probably using crazy camera angles and all that."

"Come on, Hank. This is ten times as much blood as one body can hold, and you know it. Not to mention that the victim only has an eye and a stomach wound. They'd eventually bleed out, but they aren't going to spray all over the road like this. The artistry is impressive. I'll give them that. But if we were investigating this particular crime scene, we'd know immediately that there was more to the story than we'd been told."

"In this scene, yes, we were taking a stylized approach," said Justin. "But if you two wanted to be our consultants, we could really use your expertise."

The officers exchanged a look.

"We're supposed to be doing some community outreach anyway," said Officer Hank. "I think this qualifies."

"If a real crime is committed, we'll have to leave obviously, even if it's in the middle of a shot," said the second officer. "Saving real people has to take priority over killing fake ones."

"I completely understand."

"Who wants a hug?" asked Mr. Pamm, walking around in his bloody suit with open arms. He was in a weirdly jolly mood. Maybe he'd been angry all of this time because nobody ever invited him to participate in something cool.

"Thanks, Bobby," said Justin. "You did great."

"I'm traumatized forever."

"No, you're fine. But the scene will traumatize viewers forever."

"Can I take a shower now?"

"No. Uncle Clyde doesn't have a working shower in his home anymore. Thanks to the cops being here, lots of his neighbors are watching what's happening, so your job is to get all of those gawkers to play zombies."

"I can still feel the syrup running down the back of my shirt."

"Man up," Justin told him. He waved Spork over. "I want you to get footage of this true hero. He didn't risk his life, but when that syrup dries all over his body, it's going to be really itchy and uncomfortable. And he didn't complain even once."

"Half of today's footage is of him complaining," said Spork.

"We'll bleep it out. Not many people would make this kind of sacrifice for the art. I sure wouldn't have let anybody pour that much blood on me or chew on real sheep guts. Bobby did. And for this, I salute him."

"I salute you, Bobby," said Spork.

"I'll go see if I can get more zombies," said Bobby, walking away.

Spork pointed the camera at Justin. "So after your first big shot of the day, how are you feeling?"

Justin smiled. "For the first time, I feel like we're achieving true greatness."

26

BOBBY GOT ANOTHER TEN PEOPLE TO AGREE TO be zombies. And miraculously they found a thirteen-year-old girl named Cindy who wanted to go to a beauty academy someday, so they put her to work making up the background zombies, the ones who didn't need gruesome appliances stuck to their faces.

Alicia and Christopher were here to shoot the final scene of the movie. Not the last scene they had to shoot *for* the movie— there were so many scenes left that whenever he thought about it, Justin's stomach dropped like he was plummeting down the first hill of a roller coaster—but the final dramatic shot, where Veronica Chaos and Runson Mudd stood together on a street littered with the countless zombies they'd killed and the camera slowly pulled back until the screen cut to black. This would be followed by the best part of the entire movie, namely the credit that said, "Directed by Justin Hollow."

Okay, they weren't just standing together.

They were kissing.

Justin was not a fan of the kissing scene.

"It's too predictable," he'd said. "If two people have fallen in love, the audience is going to expect them to kiss, so why don't we subvert expectations and have them *not* kiss?"

"So…what? You want the payoff to their whole relationship to be them doing a fist bump?"

"Why can't they just gaze dramatically off into the horizon? That's what I'd be doing in their situation. I'd be looking boldly toward the future, not trying to snog somebody."

"We've already discussed this," Gabe had said. "It's a kiss between two actors playing fictional characters we created for them. If you can't handle that, you shouldn't be a director."

And so Alicia, lovely Alicia, and Christopher were standing in the middle of the street, covered in blood, while the actors playing zombies lay on the pavement. A couple of them had asked for pillows, but Justin had explained that it stretched credibility too much for them to have been killed and then fallen on top of a comfy pillow. Uncle Clyde went around, dousing them with blood and scattering body parts all over.

"Camera ready?" Justin asked Gabe.

"Ready."

"Slate."

Daisy did her slate, once again without pinching anything in the clapboard.

"Action!"

Gabe very slowly began to walk backward.

Alicia and Christopher had no lines. This was where the final music would swell. All they had to do was turn to each other, look into each other's eyes, and then share a gentle kiss.

They turned to each other.

Looked into each other's eyes.

Leaned into each other.

And shared a gentle kiss.

A gentle kiss that seemed to be going on a bit long, but that was okay. Justin wasn't jealous. Honestly their lips were barely even touching, and he thought he might have even detected a faint trace of disgust in Alicia's expression. It was probably because of the blood instead of the person she was kissing, but Justin would take the disgust any way he could get it.

"Whoops," said Gabe. "Aw, jeez, I'm sorry."

"What?"

"I stumbled over something. We'll have to do it again."

"Are you serious?"

"Yeah, it's hard to walk backward and keep the shot steady. I'm really sorry." Gabe looked genuinely apologetic. This betrayal had not been on purpose. That didn't mean Justin forgave him, but at least it had been an accident.

"All right," said Justin, remaining professional. "How about we practice the shot without the kissing part a few times just to make sure this doesn't happen again?"

"No, it's okay," said Gabe. "There was a severed hand on the ground."

"We should practice anyway. It's disrespectful to the actors if we make them repeat shots multiple times because we on the crew aren't fully prepared."

"We're fine," said Christopher. "We'll do as many takes as you want."

"Back to your places then. Camera ready?"

"Ready."

"Slate."

Daisy did the slate. Even though Justin was all business on the set, he really didn't understand how she could keep doing the slate without at least once pretending that she'd pinched her nose in it. Everybody enjoyed that joke.

"Action!"

Gabe began to walk backward again.

Alicia and Christopher turned to each other, gazed into each other's eyes, and shared a gentle kiss.

Then it stopped being such a gentle kiss.

"Ow!" said one of the zombies who'd asked for a pillow. He sat up, clutching his leg. "Leg cramp!"

"Is he in the shot?" Justin asked Gabe.

Gabe stopped walking. "Yeah."

"Cut!"

Alicia and Christopher separated, though not as quickly as Justin would have preferred.

"You're out of the scene," Justin told the zombie.

"You try lying on the pavement without getting a leg cramp!"

"Go. You can still have cookies, but I need you out of my shot."

The zombie stood up and limped out of the shot.

"Anybody else getting leg cramps?" Justin asked.

"My legs are fine," said one of the zombies, "but this liver by my head is really distracting. Can somebody move it?"

"No. The liver stays."

"Can it at least not be glistening?"

"All right, fine. Anybody who is uncomfortable with the internal organs lying next to them is welcome to move, but do it now."

Several of the zombies moved to new places on the street.

"Does it still look like the aftermath of a zombie massacre?" Justin asked Gabe.

Gabe peered through the camera. "Yeah, we're good."

"Action!"

Alicia and Christopher turned to each other, gazed into each other's eyes, and went straight into a passionate kiss.

Gabe slowly walked backward.

The heroine and hero put their arms around each other, still kissing. Justin watched them carefully, ready to call, "Cut!" if he saw any tongue.

"Wow, they're really going at it," Uncle Clyde whispered.

"Shhhh."

"Should I call one of the fire engines back so we can turn the hose on them?"

"Seriously. Shhhh."

"I see saliva."

Justin looked over at Gabe, making very sure that there was nothing behind him that might cause him to stumble. There was absolutely no way they were doing this scene again. If the final scene of their movie involved the cameraman tripping, so be it.

"Do we have the shot?" Justin asked.

Gabe shook his head and continued walking backward.

Alicia and Christopher were even making soft moaning sounds while they kissed. What was wrong with them? Who told them to relate so well to their characters?

Justin's face burned, and it was probably even redder than the faces of the people who were covered in blood. But he would not call, "Cut!" until Gabe had the complete shot. He was a professional. He was not jealous. He was not jealous. He was not jealous.

He was not jealous.

He, Justin Hollow, was not jealous.

Justin Hollow, director of this movie, was not jealous.

He was not jealous.

He was not jealous.

Maybe he felt a smidgen of mild envy. But not jealousy.

Not jealousy. Not jealousy. Not jealousy. Not jealousy.

Hank the police officer chuckled. "If they keep this up, I may have to arrest them for indecent behavior."

Was Christopher dipping her? It looked like he was dipping her a little. This was unacceptable! A gentle kiss! That's what Justin had instructed them to do! Didn't they realize that he'd have to watch this over and over during the editing process? It was cruel and unusual punishment!

Couldn't Gabe walk backward any faster? Why did the camera need to pull back slowly for their final shot? What was wrong with the camera pulling back quickly? Audiences didn't need to watch those two going at it like slobbering beasts.

"She's kneading his back," Bobby whispered. "Was she supposed to do that?"

"No, she was not."

"See, you were all worried that they wouldn't have any chemistry, but that's the most chemistry I've ever seen in my life."

"No, I said that they *would* have chemistry."

"Oh. Well, you were right. Because look at them!"

"You do remember that I have feelings for Alicia, right?"

"Still?"

"Yes!"

"Oh, I thought you were over that. So everything I've been saying for the past fifteen seconds has sounded really heartless. I'm sorry about that, though it kind of serves you right for making me eat the eyeball."

"I made you chew the eyeball, not eat it."

"I accidentally swallowed it when I put the intestine in my mouth. I wasn't going to say anything unless I started choking."

"Can we have this discussion later?"

"Yeah, sure thing."

"And…I've got it," said Gabe.

"Cut!" said Justin.

Alicia and Christopher did not separate.

"Cut!" Justin repeated.

Their lips remained locked together.

Okay, enough was enough. Justin understood the good fortune Christopher was experiencing right now, but it wasn't appropriate to stand there, slobbering all over each other after the director called, "Cut!" twice. If they wanted to keep going at it, they could at least have the courtesy to crawl down into burnt ruins of Uncle Clyde's basement so nobody else would have to witness their animalistic cravings.

Justin stormed over to them. "So hey, remember that time a few seconds ago that I called, 'Cut?' It's something we film directors say to indicate that the on-camera action no longer needs to continue. I assumed that you were aware of this, but perhaps a reminder is necessary. Maybe I could get the production designer to come up with some visual aids. Oh, wait. We don't have a production designer, so I guess you'll have to figure out on your own that when I say… Hey, are you two okay?" Justin stopped the flow of sarcasm as he realized that Christopher was frantically gesturing to their lips.

Christopher said something that was muffled. Alicia added something that was equally muffled.

"Hey, Uncle Clyde? Could you come here a second. I think the fake blood dried, and they can't get their lips apart."

Uncle Clyde rushed over and looked at them. "Yep, that's what happened all right."

"Well, fix it."

"Hand me the rubbing alcohol."

"Where is it?"

"You brought some, right?"

"No, I assumed you had it."

"Mine was lost in the fire. It might have been what caused the fire actually. That stuff is pretty flammable."

"You two aren't suffocating, right?" Justin asked.

Alicia and Christopher shook their heads as one.

"Should we try to pull them apart?"

"Nope," said Uncle Clyde. "That's a good way for one of them to lose a set of lips. Believe me. You don't want the legal hassles that go with that kind of thing."

"Do any of you zombies have rubbing alcohol?"

One of the female zombies sat up. "I've got a bottle, but it's at home. I only live a few houses down. I'll go get it."

"Thanks."

The zombie hurried off. Justin wasn't sure if he should continue to be consumed with jealousy over the Alicia-Christopher situation. Probably not. They didn't seem to be having a very good time.

"I know you've got an issue right now," said Gabe, "but the shot looks fantastic. Totally worth it. Assuming, y'know, that there's no permanent damage to their lips."

The rubbing alcohol did the trick. When Alicia and Christopher's lips came apart, Justin got the impression that neither one of them was in any rush to attempt another kiss.

Justin knew that it was evil for him to be happy about this, but sometimes you just had to be evil.

"MAKE SURE YOU GET A CLOSE-UP OF THE LOGO," said Justin.

"I am," Gabe assured him, zooming in on the Monkey Burger sign.

"It needs to look appealing."

"It's completely appealing."

"Go inside and get a few shots of people enjoying their food. Try not to get any close-ups of the actual food because it never looks edible, but get seven or eight shots of smiling faces."

"Do you want me to ask somebody to rub their tummy in satisfaction?"

"No. If they ask what you're doing, say that you're getting footage for one of those restaurant shows. Tell them that later today the host is going to take the Monkey Burger challenge and eat a twelve-pound burger in half an hour. Nobody will leave if they think they'll get to witness that."

"I'll be back." Gabe went inside with the camera.

"Are you about ready?" Justin asked Christopher.

Christopher applied some more ChapStick. "Yeah."

They were about to shoot a flashback sequence showing

Runson Mudd's first encounter with the living dead. The crowd of zombies stood behind Justin, waiting for their cue.

Since they'd had so much difficulty recruiting extras, Justin had decided that perhaps they should utilize actors who were not necessarily aware that they were in a movie. It was entirely possible that one or both of the police officers would have discouraged this, but fortunately they'd been called away to investigate an armed robbery.

The owner of Monkey Burger was okay with the scene as long as the film didn't try to imply that human flesh tasted better than his hamburgers. Justin had assured him that it wouldn't.

"And if any of the zombies are eating guts, you need to make it clear that these are guts from a person and that they're not eating a burger. I don't want potential customers thinking that our burgers look like guts."

"They won't."

"And you can't do a scene where a zombie is eating guts and then changes his mind and starts eating a burger instead," the owner had said. "That sounds like it's a compliment, but it's still too close of an association between our burgers and human guts. If I see that on the big screen, you'll be hearing from my attorney."

"It's time," Justin said to Christopher. "Go in, sit down, and act natural."

Christopher applied one last layer of ChapStick and went into the restaurant.

"Listen up, zombies," said Justin. "It's very important that we get this in one take, so please no giggling, no matter how hilarious the customers' terror is. Do *not* bite anybody for real. I repeat, do *not* bite anybody. Some of the customers may have pepper spray, so I need all of you to be on high alert. Don't knock any trays of food to the floor if customers are still eating because we'll have to buy them new lunches then. Are there any questions?"

"Is the production insured in case somebody gets injured?" asked one of the zombies.

"Yes," said Uncle Clyde. "I've taken care of it."

"It's almost time to go in," said Justin. "Everybody clear your mind except for zombie thoughts. Let's hear your zombie groans."

The zombies groaned.

"Perfect. And…action!"

The zombies shuffled toward the restaurant. The one in front helpfully held the door for the others, but fortunately that polite-but-inappropriate-for-a-zombie act wouldn't be caught on camera.

Justin, Bobby, Daisy, and Uncle Clyde waited patiently for the first scream.

Somebody screamed.

Then somebody else screamed.

A woman came running out of the restaurant.

"Catch her! Catch her!" Justin told Bobby. "Make her sign a release form!"

Bobby hurried after the woman.

A man walked out of the restaurant, shielding the eyes of a young boy. Daisy went after him with another release form.

"How many people do you think will believe that this is the real zombie apocalypse?" asked Uncle Clyde.

"Not too many. I just want them to look startled."

"Maybe they'll play along."

"I hope so."

The screams continued.

"Yeah, they're playing along," said Justin. "Cool."

"Or else your zombies are getting too much into their roles."

"I instructed them not to."

"If I'm in full zombie makeup and I've psyched myself up and some lady is holding her arm in front of her face, I don't care what the director said. I'm going for the arm."

"I think they'll be responsible."

More screaming.

"The customers are good actors," Justin noted.

"They certainly are."

"Maybe I should go in there."

"You'll get in Gabe's shot."

"This is the end of days!" a woman wailed.

Justin relaxed. "She's just playing along."

"You sure?"

"Yes. That sounds like movie dialogue. That's not something anybody would actually say in this situation in real life."

Additional screams.

"Run for your lives from the zombie menace!" a man shouted. "We're all *doooooomed*!"

"Okay, good. That's definitely somebody playing along. The zombies didn't get out of control." Justin frowned. "I wish he was a better actor though. I hope he's not messing up the scene."

There was the sound of glass breaking.

"Ummmm…" said Justin.

"Was anybody supposed to break glass?"

"No."

"I don't see any shattered windows. Maybe a server dropped something."

"Even so, that's not good. We don't want people walking on glass."

"Yeah, I'd better call cut." Justin ran toward the restaurant. "Cut! Cut! *Cut!*"

Nobody was injured in the attack on Monkey Burger. A glass of water did get shattered, and three burgers were dropped on the floor. But overall the customers seemed to have been entertained, and all of them cheerfully signed release forms. It wouldn't have made sense to blur somebody's face in a movie, so if some people had refused to let themselves appear on screen, Justin would have digitally decapitated them.

The attack on the clothing store also went well. The lady who'd been in the fitting room did refuse to sign the form. But they could edit around her, and it was her own fault for rushing out to see what the commotion was about before she was ready.

The attack on the doughnut shop suffered a setback when an elderly woman was a bit too quick on the draw with her Taser. Though the zapped zombie was cool about it, after he stopped twitching, Justin decided that they'd pushed their luck far enough.

"How do you feel about today's material so far?" asked Spork, filming Justin at such an angle that he worried about his nostrils being sufficiently clean.

"It's great. Maybe it's kind of cheesy if you watch the raw footage, but once we edit it together and add music, it will be true horror."

"So do you think that you're making the greatest zombie movie ever?"

"It's hard to say."

"If it turns out to not be the greatest zombie movie ever, will you feel like you've failed?"

"No. If it turns out to be the worst zombie movie ever, yeah, I might feel like I've failed. Because even the biggest zombie fan in the world has to admit that when you're talking about the worst zombie movie ever, the bar is *really* low. In fact, it would probably be harder to make the worst zombie movie ever on purpose than it would to make the best one."

"Maybe you should try that."

"No, no, I'd rather make a good one."

Spork went off to interview somebody else. Justin was really pleased, but deep in his heart—actually even on the surface of his heart—he knew that they weren't making an all-time zombie classic. But at least they were *trying* to make something great. How many fifteen-year-olds actually completed a feature film?

Not that he could put himself into that category yet. They were so far behind schedule that he couldn't even conceive of a way they could finish on time, unless everybody was willing to skip school for two weeks and fail their final exams. They weren't. He didn't even have to ask to know that they weren't.

Nor was he. It felt good to realize that this project wasn't entirely all-consuming and that he still cared about his non-movie future.

The only way to finish was to do something drastic. To not only take away the safety net but to raise the tightrope by about two hundred feet. And take away the pole that tightrope walkers use for balance. And make them wear boots filled with rocks. And then hang a bunch of yetis from the rope.

He had an idea, but Gabe was going to freak.

"What?" said Gabe, not freaking out but also not saying, "What?" in a particularly merry tone of voice.

"We do the whole final sequence in one shot."

"That's the last third of the script."

"Right."

"That's half an hour," said Bobby.

"Also right."

Gabe gave Justin an incredulous look. "We can't do half an hour in one unbroken shot."

"If we pull this off, then we've got time to finish the rest of the movie! And you'll get credit for an amazing technical feat."

"The last half hour of the movie has stunts. Special effects. It takes place all over the school."

"Right. In the new version, we follow Alicia and Christopher the whole time. They're good at staying in character. We follow them through the whole school, fighting off zombies."

"What about the blood? If we do it in a single take, nobody can wipe up the blood. Somebody will slip and hurt themselves."

"We'll add the blood later."

"We said no CGI blood."

"Did you see how much blood got dumped on Bobby and Mr. Pamm? If somebody watches our movie and complains about insufficient blood, that's just them being unhappy with their own lives. I have faith in you, Gabe. You can do this. You can keep it in focus."

"What if somebody really messes up?"

"If that happens, we'll cover it with a digital shot of a zombie walking in front of the camera. I'm not promising you that it will turn out great. But if it works, this will be our hook! This will be what makes people want to see the movie!"

"There is a ninety-nine percent chance that this will be laughably bad."

"I'll take those odds."

"Those are terrible odds."

"But if it works…"

"Yes, on the one-in-a-hundred chance that it's not embarrassingly bad, it'll be pretty cool. But you don't understand how much work goes into an extended single take. You don't just improvise something like that. It takes tons of rehearsal. You have to know exactly where the camera needs to be at every moment. You have to figure out how to light the scene properly but keep the lights out of the shot. How are we going to get everybody through a doorway? Have you worked that out? Will our movie still be great if the camera is stuck behind a long line of zombies waiting to get through a doorway?"

"No," said Justin. "It will not still be great. I'm asking you to trust me. Not to trust me that it will work. I'm fully admitting that it will probably be an epic disaster. I'm asking you to trust me that we should take the risk on the one percent chance that it *does* work and we make magic. If we don't make magic, are we really any worse off?"

"I guess not. But I want it stated for the record that Bobby dropped a boom mic on our lead actress in a very simple shot that was only fifteen seconds."

"He's right," said Bobby. "I did."

"I understand that. And I believe he can do better."

"I believe he can too," said Gabe. "But I do want my comment on the record."

"It's on the record," said Spork.

"So we're going to try this," said Justin. Neither Gabe nor Bobby had officially agreed, but he figured that if he moved forward as if they had, they might not protest. "I need you guys to work with Uncle Clyde on touching up the zombie makeup. Some of their wounds are starting to fall off. The maintenance guy is going to meet me at school to let me in, so make sure everybody is there in half an hour."

"I'll go with you," said Gabe.

"No, that's okay. I've got this covered."

"What if you need to carry something?"

"I won't. It'll be fine. The zombies are more important."

Gabe narrowed his eyes. Justin wanted to chuckle in a manner that deflected suspicion, but he wasn't confident enough in his chuckling abilities to try.

"I'll take Spork with me," said Justin.

"All right. We'll meet you at school."

28

"MY NAME IS JUSTIN HOLLOW. THIS IS MY VIDEO confession. If you are watching this, we got busted breaking into the school, and I want to make it clear that nobody else associated with the motion picture *Dead Skull,* coming soon to a theater near you, is aware of this scheme. As far as they know, we have permission to be here. I've been really busy with this movie, and I haven't had a chance to research exactly how illegal this is. But I'm a student at the school, and we're not going to break anything. And we'll clean up when we're done, so I'm hoping that it's no big deal. Nevertheless, I want to take full responsibility for the whole trespassing thing just in case. Thank you for your time."

Justin shut off the camera and handed it back to Spork.

"I can't believe you made me an accomplice," said Spork. "That's so cool."

"You have plausible deniability," Justin told him. "As far as I'm concerned, you were never here. If we get caught, I'll say that I took your camera when you weren't looking. If we don't get caught, I'll upload the video to my computer and then delete it from your camera just so that nobody asks why you didn't say anything when you found the video. But we'll only need to worry about that if we leave behind some evidence and get caught after the fact."

"Are you guys about done?" asked Patrick.

"Yeah. Go ahead and break in."

"I'm not breaking in. I've got keys. My dad's a custodian."

"Oh. Does that mean we're actually allowed to go inside?"

"No, it's still trespassing." Patrick unlocked and opened the side door. "There you go." He propped it open, picked up his backpack, and then walked inside.

"Wait," said Justin. "You can't do any vandalism while we're here. We already talked about this."

"It's not vandalism if it's artistic."

"No, really. We can't mess with anything. No graffiti."

"I can't be in the school after hours without creating some graffiti. I'm sorry."

"Won't your dad have to be the one to clean it up?"

"He'll get over it."

"There can't be any evidence that we were here."

"Won't the movie itself be evidence?"

"Yes, but by then nobody will care. I just don't want to get caught before it's finished."

Patrick jiggled his backpack, which rattled as if it were full with cans of spray paint. "I don't know…"

"I'll make it up to you. I promise. I guarantee complete graffiti satisfaction. You just can't do it tonight, okay?"

"All right."

"Thank you for unlocking the school for me."

"No prob. Don't hurt any fish."

"I won't."

Patrick left. Breaking into the school after dark didn't feel as deliciously naughty as Justin might have hoped, but then again he'd never aspired to become part of the town's criminal element. They were going to get the shot and leave.

He walked through the hallway and turned on the lights. The school was actually kind of creepy when he was there all alone. Even the football trophies were a little unnerving, and he'd never noticed the haunted look in the eyes of their bumblebee mascot.

There were lots of doors and lots of places for zombies to spring out. Honestly, Veronica Chaos and Runson Mudd were not very bright for choosing this place for their final stand against the zombies.

This scene would work. It had to work.

"It'll work," said George A. Romero, director of *Night of the Living Dead*. Justin could see right through him like Obi-Wan Kenobi. "You just have to believe in yourself."

"Are you sure?" asked Justin. "A lot of my problems seem to be because I believed in myself too much."

"You can do this," said Sam Raimi, wearing a transparent *Army of Darkness* T-shirt. "I don't say that about everyone. Some people *can't* do it. And I tell them that to their face, and then I laugh at their tears. But not you, Justin. Not you."

"There's no way you'll mess this up," said a conjured Peter Jackson. "When I made *Dead/Alive* all those years ago, nobody thought I'd go on to make a multibillion-dollar hobbit franchise. Now I could have all of my enemies killed if I wanted. And I do want. And I have. But you shouldn't because it's wrong."

"They're all right," said a glowing and see-through Penny Marshall. "I've never made a zombie movie, and I don't have any plans to start now. And you're too young to remember me from *Laverne & Shirley* or even *A League of Their Own…*"

"I've seen *A League of Their Own*."

"Really?"

"Yeah."

"What did you think?"

"It was great."

"Thank you. Anyway, this scene will be fine. Talk to you later."

The directors vanished.

This was it. This was Justin's moment to show that he had what it took to be a legendary film director. This was his time to make people say, "Holy cow, if this is what he can do at fifteen, what will he be doing when he's thirty-six?"

This was Justin's moment of glory.

Or this was his time to prove that if his moment of glory got all screwed up, he'd handle it well.

"Think of it like a really big fun house," Justin told Alicia and Christopher. "You're going to walk through slowly for maximum suspense, and occasionally zombies will jump out at you. Do not hit them with anything. Do not throw anything at them. Do not punch or kick them. These zombies are to be shot only. If a zombie doesn't drop the first time, keep pretending to shoot it until it does."

"We don't get to kick any zombies?" Christopher asked.

"You'll get to kick plenty of zombies later," said Justin. "But these won't have padding."

"That's reasonable."

"Question," said Alicia. "When I walk by my locker, is it okay if Christopher asks me whose locker that is? Then can I say that I have no idea? Like an inside joke?"

"I'd rather you didn't, but if you feel you must, I'll allow it."

"What if I just do a sideways glance at it and raise an eyebrow?"

"Same answer."

"I'll see how I feel in the moment."

"That's fine. Is everybody ready?"

Everybody in the hallway indicated that they were ready. The zombies, who were hiding around the school, were not available to answer the question, but Justin was confident that they were ready as well. He would have loved (*loved!*) to use the principal's intercom as his means of communicating with the cast and crew, but he had to keep his vow not to mess with school property.

Daisy did the slate.

"Action!" said Justin.

Alicia and Christopher walked down the hallway slowly, cautiously, ever-vigilant for zombies. Bobby followed them with the boom mic, and Gabe followed them with the camera.

"Cut," said Justin.

Alicia looked back at him.

"Somebody's shoes are squeaking."

"I think it's yours."

Justin took off his shoes and set them against the wall. "Can somebody please make sure I don't leave without those?" He was relatively certain that he wouldn't accidentally leave the school without his shoes, but that would be such a shameful way to get caught that he didn't want to take the risk.

"Action!"

They followed Alicia and Christopher down the hallway

again. Gabe's arm was rock-steady as he held the camera. Bobby's arm was not quite rock-steady as he held the boom mic, but it didn't dip down into the shot.

As they reached the end of the hallway, Alicia put her hand on the knob to the door leading to Room 131, the site of many a frightening encounter with home economics. She very slowly turned the knob and then very slowly pushed the door open. She turned on the light.

Inside the room there was nothing.

Well, there was stuff, just no zombies.

She and Christopher walked into the room very slowly to build suspense. Gabe, Bobby, Justin, Daisy, and Spork followed them, being careful not to make any noise or cast any reflections. These smooth school floors were not ideal for walking around in socks. If Justin slipped and fell, he wasn't sure if he should try to land on his left arm and break it worse or land on his right and have two broken arms.

Alicia and Christopher continued walking through the room in a suspense-building manner. Nothing continued to happen because nothing was supposed to happen until the third room.

"Cut," said Justin.

Everybody looked at him.

"Is it just me, or is this is boring as crap?"

"It is kind of boring," Bobby admitted.

"Yeah, it's boring," said Christopher.

"Very boring," said Spork.

"I've been less bored," said Daisy.

"The only reason I didn't scream out in boredom is because I didn't want to mess up the shot," said Gabe.

"I was too focused on my performance to judge," said Alicia.

Justin sighed. "This won't work. We can't do this for half an hour. What were we thinking?"

"*We?*" asked Gabe.

"Bobby, go round up the zombies."

"I just put them in their rooms!"

"We need them all in one hallway. Veronica Chaos and Runson Mudd can fight their way through a thick horde of them."

"You don't have to use my character's full name every time if you don't want to," said Christopher. "I know we're trying to speed things up."

Bobby left to gather the zombies. Justin felt bad about ditching his astounding technical achievement of a final shot, but he was proud of himself for realizing that it wasn't working before he wasted any more time. That was the sign of an excellent director—knowing when to finally accept that the person who had earlier warned you that something was a bad idea was correct.

When they walked out of the home economics room, Justin noticed that his shoes were gone.

"What happened to my shoes?" he asked.

"They're over there," said Gabe, pointing to them. "Right where you left them. You were looking the wrong way."

"Oh. Yeah, okay, I see them now. The school looks a lot different when you're here without..." Justin almost said, "without permission," but fortunately he managed to prevent himself from finishing the dumbest sentence he'd started to say in a long time during an era of his life when a great many of his sentences weren't brilliant.

He walked over to retrieve his shoes, hoping that Gabe wouldn't ask him to say the remaining words.

By the time he put on his shoes plus another twenty-eight

minutes, Bobby had brought all of the zombies back to the hallway. Many of them looked annoyed, but Justin chose to believe
that it was simply because of their makeup.

"I apologize for making you sit alone in a classroom waiting
for a camera crew that never showed up," said Justin. "I appreciate
your continued patience. Rest assured that every one of you will
get your name on the screen by itself during the opening credits."

"Say what?" asked Gabe.

"I've decided that zombies work better in large groups. A
pretty obvious part of the zombie mythos, I'll admit, but like I've
said many times since I began this venture, I'm very tired. So I
need you all to channel your inner corpse and be as scary as possible. I want to hear moans that chill me to my very core. Those
of you with rotted fake teeth and the guy with real ones, I want
your mouths open as wide as possible. I want your eyes to look
so frightening that we don't need to digitally replace them, even
though we will anyway. I want to feel the absolute unimaginable,
nightmarish agony of being dead!"

One of the zombies raised his hand.

"Yes?"

"I thought this was going to be a fun movie."

"No, it's unrelenting horror."

"Gotcha. May I be excused?"

"Yes. Turn in your chin gash to Bobby on the way out. The
rest of you, this is your moment! This is the reason you've given
up a perfectly good Saturday to be with me, and this is the reason
you won't mind when I tell you that you'll need to sleep in your
makeup because we still need you tomorrow, and we can't afford
to redo your faces. This is your chance to live forever. Most people
don't get this chance. I think we all know somebody who was

long forgotten. That won't be you. I'm not promising to make movie stars out of all of you, but in two hundred years, when civilization has crumbled to dust and been replaced by a newer, better civilization, somebody will excavate a Blu-ray player. And in that Blu-ray player will be a copy of *Dead Skull* or whatever we end up calling it. And they'll watch the movie, and *you will be remembered*!"

One of the zombies applauded. The others didn't join in, so the zombie stopped applauding and looked sheepishly down at his feet.

"So be scary, my zombie friends. Be scary! When I call, 'Action!' I want to experience genuine fear! I want to capture the true essence of the living dead on the silver screen! You and you and you and you and all of you—please don't take it personally if I didn't point to you individually because I was just going left to right—you are going to make me proud! You are going to make millions of zombie fans happy! You are going to make millions of non-zombie fans into zombie fans! You are going to make millions of people who have no particular opinion about zombie movies into people who *do* have an opinion about them! This is your destiny!"

"I was with you until you said the destiny part," said one of the zombies. "That's taking it a bit too far. I'm starting to feel like you're patronizing us."

"Nothing could be further from the truth. If anything, I'm not emphasizing your destiny enough! I'll drop it if that's the way you all feel, but I really was working toward something big with this."

"I wasn't trying to speak for everybody," said the zombie. "I apologize if that's the way it sounded. Please continue."

"I've kind of lost my momentum. Oh well. All I'm saying is that I want to be *terrified*!"

And when Ms. Weager walked around the corner, Justin felt all of the fear he desired.

29

THE BIGGEST PROBLEM WITH TRYING TO INSPIRE A group of zombies to be as frightening as possible was this: When your principal showed up to investigate the report that unautho-rized students were making a zombie movie in the school, the zombies were so worked up to express their zombie nature that they pretended they were going to eat her.

Ms. Weager was not the most receptive audience to this.

It was very unlikely that she believed they were real zombies that were going to devour her flesh even in the moment. She probably just thought they'd gone berserk and were trying to take a bite out of her arm like a rabid person might. Either way, she fell to the ground, shrieking.

If somebody had said, "Hey, Justin, one day Ms. Weager is going to be surrounded by zombies, and she'll be on the floor screaming her head off!" Justin would have said, "Ha-ha! I bet that will be an amusing sight for sure! I look forward to that day!" To an uninvolved spectator, it probably was a delightful thing to witness, but for somebody as emotionally involved as Justin, it was stomach-churning terror.

"Stop!" he shouted.

Ms. Weager's fright was short-lived. Her next reaction, after she stood back up, was to start knocking zombie heads together.

Three pairs of zombies were down before she stopped.

Gabe dropped the borrowed camera, which broke into four pieces.

"Hey, Ms. Weager, are you here to be in our movie?" asked Bobby.

"Cut," said Justin.

"You never said, 'Action,'" Alicia informed him.

"I know. Just…cut."

Justin sat in Ms. Weager's office with his parents, who were not happy to be there.

Everybody else had been sent home. None of them seemed to be big fans of Justin as they left.

"Mistakes were made," Justin admitted.

"Mmm-hmm," said Ms. Weager.

"I don't know what to say. I take full responsibility for this."

"We knew he was excited about this movie," said Mom. "We didn't know it would lead to misdemeanors."

"Can you give me one good reason why I shouldn't expel you?" Ms. Weager asked.

"Yes," said Justin. "Given time I can."

"Do you know what I think should happen?"

"No, ma'am."

"I think you should be suspended for two weeks. This means you'll miss all of your final exams and have to take your freshman year over again."

Dad stiffened. Mom put her hand over her mouth but didn't quite block the sob.

"That's, uh, yeah, that's harsh," said Justin. "I did come up with the reason why you shouldn't expel me. We didn't break anything."

"That remains to be seen when we check the lock you say you picked. Besides, we're now discussing suspension, not expulsion. Best-case scenario for you is that you make the classes up in summer school."

Justin's face burned like Uncle Clyde's house.

Ms. Weager leaned back in her chair. "When I was your age, I was impulsive. Even a little reckless. I had that spirit crushed out of me, but every once in a while, I miss it. Mr. Hollow, I am going to cut you some slack that won't be cut for you when you enter the real world. This is only because you didn't act in a malicious manner, and you didn't touch my intercom. You will remain a student here in good standing if you can prove that you didn't ignore your education in favor of the living dead."

Justin brightened. "You mean…discuss the symbolism in my movie?"

"No. I mean get As on all of your finals."

"I will. I'll do it. I promise."

This meant that he had no chance whatsoever of finishing the movie before Gabe left, but Justin felt like he was becoming more educated already, and he didn't protest.

"And the footage of me with the zombies," said Ms. Weager. "I don't expect it ever to surface."

"It won't."

"I mean it. I'm comfortable telling you right in front of your parents that I will *bury* you if anybody ever sees it."

"I understand one hundred percent," Justin said, and he meant it. Because some things just weren't worth being buried alive in a shallow grave over.

Justin threw himself upon the mercy of Gabe and Bobby, who reluctantly granted it after they watched his confession video.

"What about the movie?" asked Bobby.

"We'll finish it in the fall when Gabe gets back. Or maybe we'll change gears and make the best action movie ever. Or," he said, immediately feeling their twin glares burn into his skin, "we'll figure something out later."

"Am I in focus?" Justin asked.

"Yep," said Spork. "Ready?"

"Ready."

"Action!"

Justin grabbed his history book, opened to chapter seventeen, and began to study.

This was the first shot of what would be a thrilling studying montage.

Over the next two weeks, Spork got amazing shots of Justin sitting at his desk, highlighting passages in four different textbooks.

He got shots of Justin sitting in both the school *and* the

public library, reviewing notes with the concentration of a natural movie star.

He got more shots of Justin at his desk as Justin started reviewing the same notes he'd reviewed at the library.

He got an exciting action shot of Justin going to bed at a reasonable hour to get a full night's sleep.

He got well-framed, well-lit scenes of Justin studying with Gabe, Justin studying with Bobby, and the three of them studying together. (Admittedly that last shot was staged because there was no class that all three of them shared.)

He got shots of Justin in the lunchroom, studying while eating a nutritious lunch.

He got a quick shot of Justin moping about the fact that he hadn't seen Alicia since production on *Dead Skull* was halted, but Justin grabbed the camera from him and deleted it.

He got a shot of Justin giving the thumbs-up sign before he went in to take the first of his exams. This shot was also staged since there were two days until exams started, but he didn't want any shots of him looking like he was going to throw up.

And when they set this montage to music, it *rocked*!

And then he saw her.

It helped that she'd purposely been waiting by his locker. "When will you find out how you did?" Alicia asked.

"I already know how I did," said Justin. "It's weird. When you study and know the answers, it's a lot easier to gauge how well you did on a test."

She grinned. "Then…good. I'm proud of you."

"Thanks."

"I just want you to know that whether we finish the movie or not or however it turns out when we do finish it, I had a great time. I'll never forget it. But please finish it because I've decided that I hate my hair and I don't want to have done that for nothing."

"We'll finish it," Justin promised.

"Cool." She gave him a kiss on the cheek. "See you soon."

Would she ever decide that it was okay to date her director? Would he find some sort of sneaky loophole to change her mind? Justin didn't know. What he did know was that right now, with the sensation of her lips against his cheek still fresh and, he hoped, the remnant of some lipstick as proof, he was truly content.

30

Five months later...

"LADIES AND GENTLEMEN, WELCOME TO THE CAST
and crew screening of *Florizombies*, formerly *Dead Skull*. As you
know," said Justin, "we had some challenges in the making of
this motion picture, but I'm proud to say that we mostly kinda
finished it. You will notice some incomplete special effects and
some lighting issues, and, yes, there are some scenes that are just
voice-over narration against a black screen. We'll fix that in the
final version. Also, it's only seventeen minutes. Enjoy!"

Justin walked to the back of the theater (folding chairs in his
backyard) and stood next to Gabe and Bobby. Finally everybody
would see the result of their long hours of hard work.

"They hate it even more than we thought! Turn it off! Turn it off!"
"Don't bother turning it off! Just run!"

Epilogue

Thirteen more months later…

EVERYBODY IN THE SOLD-OUT MOVIE THEATER
applauded and cheered.

"Was that a treat or what?" asked the programming director of the Woodriver International Film Festival. "You can see
why it's won so many awards. And let's meet the filmmaker
responsible for this gem. Ladies and gentlemen, please welcome Otto Harrison!"

Spork walked to the front of the theater, waving to the crowd.

"So, Otto, what's the secret to making a documentary
like this?"

"I just point my camera and wait for the train wreck."

"Sound advice for all of you aspiring documentarians. Let's
bring out the cast!"

Justin, Gabe, Bobby, Christopher, Alicia (who'd decided to
keep the Mohawk after all, though it was now orange), Daisy,
three of the zombies, and Ms. Weager joined Spork up front.

"I've gotta say, *The Greatest Zombie Movie Ever: The Not-
Making of* Florizombies is some of the most entertaining footage

I've seen in quite a while. Admit it—the part where you accidentally blew up the car was staged, right?"

"Nope," said Justin. "Uncle Clyde did blow up his car. Fortunately nobody was hurt. He wanted me to tell everybody that he wishes he could be here, but the new *Star Wars* movie wouldn't give him the day off."

"Christopher, I understand that you're starring in the new Vin Diesel movie."

"Well, no, technically Vin Diesel is starring in it. But I'm in it."

"That's great. And Alicia…or should I say Veronica Chaos? No, I'll say Alicia. I'm sure that joke has worn thin. What are you working on now?"

"I'm in the new Justin Hollow movie."

"That's right!" said the programming director. "The big-budget zombie movie remake of your original film!"

"Low-budget," Justin corrected. "Very, very low. But it's still cool."

"It sure is. I bet your original investors never expected to get their money back and then some!"

"I assure you it did feel good to write that check."

"I can't wait to see the flick. Having seen what you, Gabe, and Bobby can't do, I'm looking forward to seeing what you can."

"Thanks. We start shooting in two weeks."

"Action!" Justin said through the megaphone.

The actors playing zombies, all six hundred of them, began

to shamble down the street. The sight was so beautiful that it brought a tear to Justin's eye.

"Don't cry," said Gabe. "You'll lose the respect of the rest of the crew."

Justin's personal assistant, Melissa, who was also his girlfriend, dabbed at the tear with a handkerchief.

Bobby watched the action in one of the monitors. He'd retired from his job as a sound engineer in favor of his role as an associate producer, which meant that he didn't really do anything but got his name prominently featured in the credits. Daisy did a much better job with the sound.

In character as Veronica K-Aws (renamed because of a rights issue), Alicia pointed her twin machine guns at the horde of zombies, smiled, and pulled the triggers.

Zombie guts began to fly everywhere, and Justin had never been happier.

Another Epilogue

BERNARD WHITTLESCUTT OPENED HIS FRONT
door, stepped outside, and froze.

Graffiti! All over his car!

Highly artistic graffiti, but still…

He looked around for the perpetrator.

A kid jumped up from behind some bushes.

"Serves you right, Stinky the Clown!" Patrick shouted before
Justin pulled him back out of sight.

Acknowledgments

You don't write a book alone. I mean, sure, you write *most* of it alone, sitting in a dark, gloomy room all by yourself. Everybody else in the entire world is out doing fun stuff, but you can't go, because you have to finish your book. As your tears drip onto the keyboard, you've never felt more alone.

Still, you don't do *everything* yourself. No matter how many times you read and re-read and re-re-read your book, there will be mistakes. So thanks to my mighty group of test readers: Tod Clark, Michael McBride, Jim Morey, Rhonda Rettig, and Donna Fitzpatrick Stinson. Thanks also to my agent, Stephanie Kip Rostan, and my agent's mighty assistant, Shelby Boyer. Thanks to Annette Pollert-Morgan, Stephanie Graham, Alex Yeadon, Kathryn Lynch, Beth Oleniczak, Chris Bauerle, Elizabeth Boyer, and the rest of the Sourcebooks crew, especially those who could sabotage this book and add "Duuuhhhh" to the beginning of every sentence.

And thanks to the whole cast and crew of the movie *Chomp*, especially writer/director/my wife Lynne Hansen. I didn't use any anecdotes from the set in this book, but maybe if I ever write a sequel…

About the Author

Jeff Strand wrote the script for the short film *Gave Up the Ghost*, which has zombies in it for a few seconds, and was an associate producer on the short zombie film *Chomp*. In the event of an actual zombie attack, he would run around crying and screaming, "We're all doomed! We're all dooooomed!" and contribute very little to everybody else's chances for survival. He's written a bunch of other books, including *I Have a Bad Feeling about This* and *A Bad Day for Voodoo*. Check out his website at jeffstrand.com.